MOY McCRORY

Bleeding Sinners

Methuen · Minerva

A Minerva Paperback

BLEEDING SINNERS

First published in Great Britain 1988
by Methuen London
This Minerva edition published 1989
by Methuen · Mandarin
Michelin House, 81 Fulham Road, London SW3 6RB

Minerva is an imprint of the Octopus Publishing Group

Copyright © Moy McCrory 1988

A CIP catalogue record for this book is available from the
British Library

ISBN 0 7493 9013 1

Printed in Great Britain
by Cox & Wyman Ltd, Reading

For Kath, Ger, Chris, Anthea and Buchi
for keeping me going while writing the book.
And Bob and Katie-Ellen.

Contents

Transubstantiation

When Bernadette Lynch woke up in the morning, an enormous potato the size of a small man lay next to her wearing her husband's pyjamas. It was the first thing she saw. She rubbed her eyes furiously. She did not want any lingering nightmares, she had no time for them; it was wash-day and she had to do the sheets.

Earlier that morning the alarm clock screamed the time. She always buried her head under the blankets. The clock was on his side of the bed, switching it off was his responsibility. Every morning it rang just after 5.30. It lost four or five minutes throughout the week and each Sunday he would reset it. It was accurate on Monday.

That morning it rang before the sky was light. He seldom rose to daylight. There was only a brief taste of that, in what she called the heart of the summer as other people might describe a lettuce, when for a small bite out of an entire year he rose to the sun. Generally his working day started in darkness. He left and returned in it. The best part of the day was kept by the factory, while the mealy bits were to be shared between them. Now there was talk of lay-offs and he had mentioned early retirement, but what he would do without the routine, she could not imagine. Even at weekends he got up early, without the alarm.

It was as if they lived on different continents, he in the dark, and she in the light. They were both used to it. She was hardly disturbed by his movements as he got ready. Most mornings she would roll over and continue to sleep. This morning she had not heard him go, but she remembered that the clock had rung longer than usual as if he had forgotten to switch off the bell.

She sat up and blinked. Each night recently she had difficulty sleeping and, occasionally, disturbed dreams, which woke her in time to watch the dawn come through the gap where the curtains did not meet. As the room gradually lightened, she would return to sleep, stretched out alone in the bed.

'It's all right for you,' he would say, 'having a lie-in every morning.'

He did not understand. Lately, the only times she could sleep were those few hours when she would stay on her own in bed, remembering how it used to be in the beginning. But not this morning. As soon as she saw the thing lying next to her she was out of the bed, shivering in her thin nightdress.

'Good God Almighty! Is someone playing a joke on me?'

She shouted for Michael, hoping he had not left, but the clock said 9.30. She had overslept and her head felt terrible.

She went into the kitchen and made a pot of tea and spent a longer time than usual draining it. She topped up her cup constantly until she had swallowed the entire potful. In a daze she let each action be determined by the one preceding it, by the slow movement of her hand and the stretch of her arm to reach the teapot. Only its emptiness made her realize that breakfast was over. She was still not dressed and she knew that it was late as she went reluctantly back to the bedroom to get her clothes.

The massive potato was still there. She had never seen anything so big. It would have won a prize at a horticultural show. It took up half the bed and seemed to have most of the blankets now. How had it got there, and why was it wearing Michael's pyjamas?

She edged quietly around the bed, trying not to make a

sound, when she knew all along that potatoes were deaf. She pulled her clothes furtively from the chair-back where she had left them the night before and, with them in a bundle, scurried to the bathroom where she locked the door before dressing. She had not done that for over thirty years, since she was first married and blushing in the daylight.

She saw herself reflected in the mirror on the cupboard. Her hair was slightly greasy at the scalp and it was lank. The perm had mostly grown out and it felt lifeless. Usually, she clipped it back from her face when it got to be in that state, before it was due to be washed. Instead, she took the bottle of shampoo out and fixing the spray to the tap, began to work up a lather. She rubbed her scalp in tiny circles until it tingled and dolloped conditioner on, sitting on the edge of the bath waiting for it to penetrate the shafts of hair. She at least tried to take care of her appearance, but her husband never bothered about himself. While she dieted and struggled to maintain her figure, he grew rounded. It did not bother him.

She looked at herself. Even with the dieting her body had thickened. The muscles of her belly were no longer tight; a small roll of fat hung over the top of her skirt when she pulled the waistband shut with the straining button. She was in better shape than him, but he was in no shape, or rather, he had become amorphous while she at least struggled to impose some order on her body.

She used to think that she could see her husband changing before her eyes, gradually taking an appearance that was more vegetable than animal. Some days, she had to stop herself from laughing when she caught him suddenly out of the corner of her eye. Now she wondered what had happened. Had Michael read her thoughts? Had he suspected her of mocking him? Was this his way of paying her back?

She rinsed the stuff from her hair and rubbed a towel over it vigorously. Already it felt better. She shook her head and the ends, where there was some perm left, sprang back into small curls. She finished dressing quickly, wishing that she could brave the bedroom to get a clean blouse, instead of the crumpled jersey which she pulled over her head, but she did not have the heart to look at the article in the bed.

She was in a state of anxiety all morning, and wore her shoes in the house as if she was on her best behaviour when visitors were coming. She even put some perfume on. The strange presence in the house made her behave the way she would among strangers. Downstairs on her own, she was still careful not to sit with her knees apart. She could not relax and at lunch-time when the phone rang, she jumped on hearing the work manager's voice.

'I was just checking that Michael was all right. Only it's odd; he's always so punctual and when he missed the bus, we thought he must be ill. In future, could one of you ring in and let us know if he's going to take time off work?'

She bluffed her way through and told him a story about Michael having a bad cold.

'I'm afraid I had to go out rather early. Michael must have fallen asleep. You know what it's like when you have a fever, don't you? Obviously he forgot to call work, so sorry.'

'Well in future, if one of you can phone in,' the work manager repeated.

'Of course,' she replied brightly, with a sinking heart.

She put the receiver back. He was not at work. What could be going on? Now she was in a muddle. Where was he? The day was becoming so confusing. 'I should have stayed in bed today,' she muttered out of habit, before she thought about what was lying up there.

Every night for thirty years she lay next to him. Of late she could not sleep so she would watch the striped pyjamas rise and fall. Sometimes she had to reassure herself that intelligent life lurked within. She had been taking a course of anti-depressants, but they kept her awake so she had thrown them out the week before. They must have been in her system, she still could not sleep. She would lie in the dark with those strange ideas which flooded her half-consciousness at 3 am.

She kept returning to their honeymoon when they spent a week in a hotel on the coast. They hardly left the room. She remembered walking along a cliff and being drenched in spray. They ran, laughing, back to the hotel. All week it was wet and raining and the sea roared outside their window. The wallpaper peeled with the constant dampness. In the bathroom there was a patch of strange, yellow fungus under the sink. But they were overheated: blood fever, a sort of madness. They did not feel the moisture on the air. Then the moment was eternal, a constant coming together of their bodies in a fearful passion which controlled their every move. It kept them awake, it started and ended to continue with the same wildness, and she knew that she was mad for it then, and mad for him throughout that week.

Fast breathing, urgency, weight of his body, staccato outbreaths, his mouth finding hers, desperate as he came inside her, their breathing in unison, their blood pounding. Pyjamas and night-dress thrown off in a frenzy, God knows where. He would hunt for them before falling asleep circling her body. In that half-light of thirty years ago, she would watch him sleeping and gently draw the top buttons together the way you would for a child.

Then she could not wait for the night, to be together with the freedom of darkness covering their bare bodies, soft and discernible to each other's fingers and mouths. She did things she could not bear to think in the clear daylight, as hard and bright it shone on her embarrassment and found their common guilt. Now, clothes muffled their slack bodies until desire was barely audible.

During the day she often played a game with herself, but it was silly and now she wished she had not. She hated

13

herself for all those times when she would imagine him growing into some other form of life. There was nothing to laugh at now.

Suppose he had really gone? People sometimes did. She remembered how, years ago, Mrs Riley vanished. They said that she went to the shops and never came home. Later, they found that all her things had gone. She had systematically taken everything which was hers, sending them ahead of her – for weeks probably – so that on the day all she needed to take was her shopping basket.

Then there was Mr Daly. He shuffled away in his carpet slippers one evening to buy a newspaper and was not heard of again until the paper ran the story the following week. Four years later, his wife received a Christmas card from him, wishing her the best for the season and asking her to drink a glass to him. There was just his name and a postmark, somewhere in Yorkshire. Mrs Daly ran out into the square screaming that she would break a glass over his neck for him, and the neighbours had to contain her and get her back indoors.

She could not believe that Michael would leave like that. There had to be some explanation. What would she say to everyone tomorrow? What would people think about it all?

'Oh, look,' they'd say, 'there's that woman, you know, the one whose husband turned into a vegetable. He's with a travelling circus now. She hardly gets to see him.'

She could do without that kind of pity.

If he had gone, all she would have to remember him by was the awful thing in the bedroom. There were some photographs, but they had been taken years before when the children were still at home. She realized that she had no image of Michael as he was, indeed the closest thing to him was the potato. She picked up the wedding photograph from the sideboard. They both looked so indecently young to be married. Yet she was not a teenage bride, she was twenty-three and he was two years older.

How had he altered so much? Thirty years put layers of fat on him, softening his angular frame and slowing him down. He differed so completely from the man in the photograph. Her husband was a shape next to her every night in bed, but once he had been slight, fast on his feet, always pushing back the lock of dark hair which fell across his clear eyes.

People went through so many stages. It was a lie to say 'adult' and leave it there as if that was a plateau of development. A foetus is all things prior to its birth. The fossilized imprint of a curled shrimp, it divides into a fish, splits into a tadpole and kicks feebly. It wears dark discs of eyes and swims in its silent underwater world, changing as each cell doubles. It arrives, a visitor to earth with its huge head, and trails the seaweed after it, still wet, from the vanished ocean. It breathes, and the same purple cord falls away unwanted, a ribbon on a birthday present.

Cell division did not stop. It went on beyond babyhood and childhood, stretching them into endless different forms. She remembered how her grandfather became more like the seed potatoes he had spent a day ridging, or he might smell of turf when he came indoors from the common bogland where he sliced the peat with his spade. Sometimes he was covered in mud past his knees. He looked as if he had been pulled up by the roots. It seemed right to put him back in the earth at the end of it all, like an old growth, shrivelled and many-eyed.

She had thought last night about cauls. Half awake, she tried to imagine what they might look like, those fine membranes of the womb's creation. Some were born with them covering the head. A good omen, midwives believed. The Victorians used to keep them, preserved inside glass covers. A horrible thought to have one on the sideboard. Attitudes had changed. Darwin's ideas triumphed at last, but they took a long time to filter through. His discoveries were laid at the feet of stiffly buttoned authorities who tried to stop the old glass cases from being smashed open.

They need not have worried; the cauls settled on the twentieth century. Her mother was a Victorian, born after the century's turn, but a Victorian no less.

When she was at school she had learnt about the immaculate conception, long before she knew what a conception was. The teacher told them that a bud grew in Mary's body, and this became a rose. It was what her own mother believed. But knowing did not make it any less marvellous.

Development: two months; opening fists, lifting the head, looking at objects close up. Four months; grasping objects, sitting up with help. Six months; beginning to sit on their own. Ten months; sitting upright and crawling.

God knows, she knew all that. She had weaned enough babies. Only it did not stop there, it went on and on throughout life, evolving slowly.

Development: after thirty years her husband was unrecognizable from the wedding photo.

And what about the brain? she thought. Wasn't it constantly active? Even when her body was asleep it sent messages to her like a radio transmitter.

Development: after thirty years she had changed too. All her beliefs had shifted, she was as different as he was.

Going back home after the honeymoon changed everything. She returned as a married woman; it ought to have given her status, instead she took up residence in the cold rented house feeling that everyone watched her, and that everyone knew. She was shocked by her week-long passion. She was ashamed in front of her mother, who looked at her too knowingly. To be so free was not correct in a woman. She wondered what had possessed her, and blamed him. He ought to have spared her that side of his nature. She had merely obeyed as a wife ought, she had done her duty. It was the pleasure that was impossible to excuse. She felt embarrassed with him; what did he think she was?

A creeping shame followed her days like a reproachful shadow and at night it crawled upon the bed beside her, castigating while she lay, waiting for some almighty judgement which would crash from the ceiling and cover her in slates, and rotten plaster.

She felt that plaster was accusatory. It absorbed shame as it did water, it swallowed feelings and set hard the memory. Even the little plaster saints on her mother's window-sill held guilt. They blushed when they saw her return, the sinful woman of the hot, lusting nights. She felt that all her family knew and she was naked in front of them.

At night she pushed him away and cried. How could he understand that now everything was dirty and horrible? She could not look in his eyes, but averted her head and gritted her teeth. Within a month she was pregnant. They had no time together really, before they had a houseful of kids. After that, she had earned her place as a woman because she had suffered horribly for her pleasure.

It could not be the same after the first birth anyway. They were always listening for a baby's crying, and at night they collapsed into bed, too tired to speak to each other.

After the last baby, she felt that the row of little plaster saints at her mother's were always watching her. When she was a child she used to talk to them, believing that they understood and listened to her. She would ask them all in turn for special intentions, and she would shift her allegiance when the current saint did not oblige her.

One afternoon, sitting in her mother's house, she could not endure their glaring, malicious eyes any longer. Her mother was upstairs watching the baby. She leapt up from the chair where she was supposed to be sleeping. Crash went Saint Jude, the patron saint of hopeless causes.

'You're hopeless now, you little grinning bastard! Put that right!'

One after the other she picked them up, smashed their heads against the sill. Saint Felicity, virgin and martyr, broken in pieces. She shouted, she screamed, until there were no saintly eyes to burn shame into her. One after the other: Blessed Martin De Porres, Saint Perpetua, cold and white, the Good Shepherd, all broken and the sill empty. She stood weeping.

'O Christ, look what I've done.'

'You've gone crackers! You're bloody mad!'

Her mother would not talk to her for days. But he must have put a word in for her because she came round soon after. She looked nervously at her daughter.

'I think you've got that . . . you know . . . thing . . . that they talk about nowadays, after having a kid, that's all. I know after I had you, all I did was cry. Every time I looked at you, I felt as if I could have cut my own wrists. But then . . . there was no name for it, they just said I was depressed. For months it went on. Some women end up hurting themselves . . . or worse.'

She looked worried, as if she was not sure who she was talking to, and whether her daughter was still a rational woman or completely mad with this modern sickness.

'It's all gone scientific now, love,' she said, rationalizing her daugher's insanity, while Bernadette knew it was one of her sanest gestures.

'I'm sorry about breaking them. I'm sorry I did that to your things. They weren't mine to do as I liked with.'

'Oh, don't worry about that,'her mother had told her, 'they were only statues. I got sick of dusting them. Anyway, you can't hurt the real saints.'

That defeated her. Her mother's faith was undented because she knew that no one could hurt those saints for her, nor chip away at the belief of years.

She hated anything to do with religion after that. She had not wanted to have the last child baptized, not because she did not believe, she believed too much. She did not want to condemn her child to another life, one was quite sufficient. He did not argue about the religious aspects, but he reminded her that the relatives would miss the knees-up, so she gave in, but she would take no part in it.

If she had been freed from something she did not feel it. The lost madness did not return; it slept, exhausted by the children. They listened through the walls, scared to make a sound in case they woke them. They became silent with each other, passion's sharpness blunted by routine.

She had no idea how it happened, but she became an atheist. A seeping disbelief edged into her vision. That day after she smashed her mother's statues, she waited for the retribution, but there was none. At school they were always told to see the priest if they were in danger of losing their faith, and they would pray for the infidel in the four corners of the earth. Now she felt the weight of her faith like a burden and was only too glad to be released from it.

They did not talk about it. She kept silent and they did not discuss many things now. Right at the beginning they had talked, trying to find out everything about each other with a hunger.

Suddenly she remembered that she had not eaten. She walked over to the table and cut a slice of bread and buttered it slowly. It was well past lunch-time, her stomach was empty yet she had no appetite. She ate the bread standing in the kitchen, the way she might when waiting for a knock on the door. She put the kettle on automatically, then switched it off. She could not face more tea. She could not finish the bread and left it on the draining-board. Out of habit she went into the hall and put her coat on.

She walked quickly out of the square, looking neither left nor right. Usually she did the shopping for something for tea, but today she could not face the local shops where people knew her. She went instead to the big supermarket near the centre. Inside, the endless rows of food piled up from floor to ceiling confused her. She stared for a long time into the freezer section, unable to make up her mind, and at the check-out her wire basket clanged emptily with only one tin in it. The label said 'Tropical Passion Fruit'. She had bought it out of perversion.

Back home she left the tin on the kitchen table and crept upstairs. Opening the door a crack, she peeped round. The potato was settled for the evening. She slammed the door and ran downstairs, her heart pounding. What could she do? She paced the hall. Outside she heard the work's bus pass, dropping men off at corners. Although she knew that Michael was not on it, still she hoped that he might walk in the door. She listened to the sound of heavy boots as they clattered on the pavement, but none stopped at her house.

It had grown quite dark. Potatoes needed that for growth. Her grandfather taught her that. Where were all the wise old men now? Every one of them dead. She wished that there was someone she could go to who would know everything.

The oldest woman in the square had the reputation of being a witch because she once told someone that she had the cure for bunions, inherited from her mother who was the seventh in line of a family of girls. Very unusual that, and they reckoned she'd been drinking the day she said it, but one of the neighbours said that her feet felt better after a visit, although she had sat with them up on a footstool for over two hours in her kitchen drinking tea. Bernadette knew that it was all superstition, but she also knew that she would pay her a visit.

At Mrs Buonito's she sat down at the well-scrubbed table.

'I'll be with you in a minute,' the woman shouted through. 'I'll just take Vincent his cup of tea.'

'How is Mr Buonito?' she asked. 'I haven't seen him about for some time now. Feet still troubling him?'

She heard the woman through the thin wall.

'It's Bernadette Lynch. . . . No, Lynch. She dropped by to say hello, see how you are . . . I said to see how you

are. . . . She's just asking after your feet . . . your feet . . .'
The loud voice said everything twice.

'Is he becoming hard of hearing then?' she asked on Mrs Buonito's return.

'I don't know, I think he hears me, but it's just that he's so far away these days, you know, dreaming. He's a bit vacant sometimes. I've got used to it. I shout when I want to catch his attention.' She smiled. 'And how are you then? How's Michael?'

'That's what I've come to see you about.'

There was a bump from the next room and Mrs Buonito jumped up. 'I'll just go and see . . .'

Bernadette went after her to help. The cup of tea had fallen from Mr Buonito's grasp and knocked on the coal scuttle. Miraculously, it had not broken. Hot tea was soaking into the carpet, rising as steam. Somehow it had missed him completely. He was sleeping upright in a chair, a colourful blanket wrapped tightly about him, and his slippers propped up on a footstool. He was absolutely still. She could see the back of his head. He was bald. That struck her as odd for he always had such wonderful thick, dark hair, from the Italian side. The last time she saw him out, although months before, he still had hair, turning to white, but plenty of it.

Mrs Buonito fussed and tucked the blanket about her husband. Bernadette picked up the cup and glanced at him over her shoulder. He was dozing with his head down, his face hidden and just the top part of his head visible.

His wife was tiny. Wiry like a sparrow, her thin legs looked as though they ought not to support her. She was struggling to heave him up because he had slumped forward. Bernadette went over to add her strength and felt grooves and bumps through the blanket. He did not seem to have any bones.

'Mrs Buonito?' she asked, feeling uncomfortable. 'Have you noticed anything strange about your husband lately. . . . I mean, has he become different?'

'Not much,' she said gaily. 'He doesn't say much any more, watches television most nights. He's stopped going out for a pint. I think it's the cold weather.'

'But, when he watches the television, I mean ... he actually watches it?'

The old woman looked at her oddly. 'Well, he might fall asleep sometimes, but he never misses an episode of "Fairley Heights".'

She looked in the paper. 'Oh, its the news, he likes the news, I'll just put it on for him,' and she switched the dial. 'When that's over I change stations and he watches that magic show, I can't stick it myself.'

There was no movement from the blanket. Then Bernadette noticed pale, transparent shoots which stuck out awkwardly from the slippers.

'Mrs Buonito?' she began, feeling suddenly afraid.

'Shall we go and finish our tea? He'll shout if he needs anything.'

She let herself be taken out to the kitchen where Mrs Buonito topped up their cups.

'Now what was it you wanted to ask me about Michael?' she asked.

Bernadette got out without once alluding to Michael's condition. If the woman was happy and had not noticed her own husband's change, she thought it was safer to leave her. Besides, she seemed genuinely fond of him the way he was, caring for him like a baby; attending his every need, carrying him to bed, safe in the knowledge that he was not out with other women.

'Oh, he's stopped all that gadding around,' she had said proudly. 'He's come to his senses in his old age. He knows I'm the one who will look after him better than anyone, and he's happy to stay at home with me.'

Bernadette left them, sitting on opposite sides of the television, the large sleeping shape and the smaller figure of Mrs Buonito, knitting a bed jacket and looking contented.

Mr Buonito had been well known for his roving eye; even she had experienced it once, many years ago. He said it was the Latin in him, and laughed. 'Always an eye for a pretty girl,' and he had winked at her.

That night she peeled the potatoes angrily. She forgot and made enough for two, gouging the eyes out ruthlessly. But she had no appetite, not with that thing lying upstairs.

She hesitated, then decided to ring up her daughter. Newly married, in the first flush, she was always panting, surprised as if she had been caught in the act.

'It's impossible,' she told her. 'That can't have happened. Are you still taking those vallium? I warned you, didn't I? Throw them out, Mam, they're doing your brain harm. People don't just turn into potatoes, not overnight. It must be some condition, there's probably a medical name for it. He could have a mild form of paralysis, or shock from something.'

She tried describing how he looked to her daughter, like something she brought home from the greengrocer's, but her daughter laughed and said that she was exaggerating. 'Those bloody pills have got you daft, you're seeing things.'

Bernadette said nothing. It was true that she could not see things clearly when she was taking the pills, her vision had been affected and her daughter was right. When she was taking them, she walked around myopically, not noticing detail, and not feeling things. She was like a sleepwalker. Possibly Michael had been a potato for a while and it was only now, when her senses were unblocked and open to the world, that she could actually see him as he was. She no longer knew.

'Are you all right Mum?' her daughter's voice sounded far off. 'I can come over tonight if you want. Do you want me to get the doctor out for Dad?'

Bernadette heard herself telling Anne that she was all

right, that she had given herself a bit of a shock, and that he was coming round. He'd just slept heavily, that was all.

'You're going to frighten the life out of me, carrying on like this,' her daughter said laughing, thinking now that it was a joke.

She decided to wait until the morning, before letting the rest of the family know.

It was much later when she finally got the nerve up to get into bed next to it. Sleep was never more out of the question. She lay watching it in the half light. She could see its head. It looked a mottled, pinkish grey, lying sideways on the pillow. But how did she know that this was its head? It was an odd growth, which burst from the purple stripes of the jacket as if one of the lines had swollen out from the too orderly pattern, distended and crazy.

Had he been swapped in the night? Was this a changeling lying next to her? If only it could have been something useful, a set of kitchen knives or an electric toaster.

She wanted to cry but could not. She felt that life was pointless. She hated what had happened to them. She wanted them to be company for each other. But it was too late. She was bored with him, but kept on as though nothing had altered. She knew that if it had been like this in the beginning, she would have run screaming and never have opted to share her life with his. They had come to this cold worn room that was their life and this time the surroundings mattered, because now they had no fever of their own to heat them.

She closed her eyes and must have dozed off, for when she opened them again she had a sense that time had passed, although it was no lighter. Something was different. She strained to hear. No birds sang. Maybe three o'clock? Michael must have opened a window because there was a fresh earthiness in the room. It was the rich smell of soil, good soil, dark for growing. She listened. There was complete silence. Not even the sound of Michael's breathing disturbed the quiet hours. Then she remembered that Michael did not have to breathe. Her hand reached out. It shook violently. Her fingers touched the shape next to her. Still the same.

She put the bedside lamp on. Her eyes smarted, blinding her initially, but as they cleared she saw the shoots which had sprouted overnight. Delicate lavender feelers, they quivered sensitively, moving towards the source of daylight and away from the harsh artificial bulb.

She pulled back the covers. Already, well established thick roots were reaching to the floor. They coiled in a heavy mass under the bed like the rope heaps stored in her grandfather's barn.

If there ever were feet, they had disappeared completely. If there ever were toes, now there were ten long shoots covered in red, loamy clay.

She thought hard. Here she was lying next to a tuber wearing her husband's pyjamas. Why didn't she feel frightened? She felt comfortable, as if she had known the vegetable all her life. It had so many of her husband's characteristics. It was just like him not to bother about getting filth everywhere, it left mud and earth all over the sheets.

She snapped the lamp off angrily, feeling irritated. She tried to pull some blanket back to cover her shoulders, but the vegetable held tight to its covers. She shivered and hunched her back against the cold.

She put her fist out and touched it again, stroked what she thought might be its back. There were no bones. Then she did something she would never have dreamed of earlier. She put out the tip of her tongue and licked the part outside the collar where Michael's neck used to be. Her mouth was full of topsoil, it was unscrubbed. It definitely was her husband, it must have grown up out of him, to change so completely and still be recognizable.

She did sleep. She dreamt strange dreams about policemen walking around the bedroom, drawing chalk marks around Michael, about having her fingerprints taken, and being interviewed and photographed. She woke up still protesting her innocence. And the potato lay against her. She had spent the night with it like an adulterous woman. It waited like an old friend, reassuring and solid.

A slow smile spread across her face. She felt as she had once before, when she was first married. Then she had been the sort of woman her mother disapproved of. She had allowed shame to crush her pleasure.

This time, she stood up, naked and strong, feeling her body coming alive. She got dressed slowly, while the eyes of the potato bored into her and she did not care.

You could say that she was emotionally attached to potatoes. Even in cities with supermarkets and the daily delivery of bread, still the potato lying in the polythene bag had the tug of earth about it. It was those summers spent in her grandparents' house with the big earthenware bowl on the table, full of steaming potatoes, plain boiled with a drop of salt. Her grandmother made the best potato bread in the world, sometimes with herbs and a bit of onion, for which she earned the reputation of being an adventurous cook.

After she was married, she learned how to cook them in every variety: baked in their jackets, par-boiled and roasted, cut into cubes and sautéd with garlic, in scallops or baked with cream. Her mouth watered.

Her grandfather never cooked a potato in his life, but he knew everything there was to know about them. He mixed up spray before the blight spores had time to settle. She would stand watching him in his navy overalls with the bit of bailer twine around his waist, and the grey felt hat he wore when working.

First, he would tip the copper sulphate crystals into the barrel. With the hose-pipe he swished in enough water to fill it up to a mark inside the tub. It took ages to pour through, and she would wait, with her instructions to turn off the tap as soon as the level started to rise. Bent over a large bowl, her grandfather would be sieving washing-soda into a thicker paste with water from the overflow barrel. He would tip this into the solution and watch it sink before stirring it with a stick. Then he would take down a clean knife kept for the purpose. Slowly he would dip this in and, for her benefit, mutter magic words, 'Sheela wheela', and make the whites of his eyes very large. Then he would pull out the knife, just as her grandmother might from the centre of a cake. Sometimes, the coppery sheen was on it and she thought that was beautiful, but that was not what he wanted and he would add more soda until the knife came out without residue.

Still the blight got in, but it could be burnt off if it was caught in time. She had seen ruined plants and recognized the look of a field about to turn: the first small spots of dark green on the leaves which grew into brown patches with their powdering of white mould. They stretched out for rows and rows, until the whole crop was lost and the field a stagnant space of slimy tops.

It had been drummed into her as a child, as it had been into them; the terrible famine of '46, and the fear of out-breeding the land. Her grandfather was a perfectionist, always ridging and furrowing so that no light got in.

'Leave a growing spud open to the light and it turns green, and there's nothing more poisonous than a green potato.'

He always sent the pigs in after harvesting, to eat up any rogues. He was a philosopher too.

'Now, look at that,' he used to say, holding up a seedling. 'Potatoes are all the same plant. We put a spud in the earth and it grows more spuds. Then we take one and put it back into the earth and it grows more. A potato is its own child, just as it is its own parent. Doesn't that make you think, now?'

He died after the lifting out, when the potatoes were lying in the field for their skins to set. They remained undisturbed for over a week, spoiled by daylight. Her grandfather's last harvest turned green and poisonous, and he had always been so careful and so proud.

She remembered the delicate white potato flowers. Once, she had dug with her hands to pull up a tuber. She gripped the base and pulled, and the clump came free from the heap, clay-coated and smelling of newly-dug graves. Early crop, sweet and yellow, their insides waxy.

There are probably much worse things a man could become, she told herself, watching the huge potato behind her in the mirror. Already she was adjusting to the idea that Michael was different. She had married him for better or for worse. People were going to alter and her own changes were as dramatic, if not as visible. Really she owed Michael an explanation of herself. This silence between them was of her making as much as his. While he would lie still and listen, she resolved to tell him everything, starting with the creeping shame that he was not responsible for. It was the first thing which came between them. She would explain about the faces of her mother's statues. She wanted to burn out all the rotting guilt while there was still time.

She knew that if she took another prescription from the doctor, her husband would resume his usual form. He would be able to catch tomorrow's bus for work and so their life would continue, with her in a daze, getting through each day without seeing. But that was no longer what she wanted. There could be no return to how things used to be, now that she could face her husband as he was.

It was the difference between them which was rare and precious. That was what she wanted to see grow. And each year when the beautiful white flowers sprouted, she would gather them together in a bunch, and they would be his gift to her.

Corpus Delicti

I have always had a fear of things changing although I know everything must. I suffer from a sense of impermanence, as though everything is shifting around me and I reach out and grasp anchors; those places which mark solid ground. I've never known another security. I'm reclusive by nature, a loner who is frightened of being alone. I put faith in places because, unlike people, they cannot move away to the next town or to the other side of the world. But even they change. I become nervous, occasionally terrified, if an old building is pulled down. I am anxious when I cannot remember what used to stand in a vacant place. If a tree that I am used to seeing is suddenly toppled I feel helpless.

I remember how last winter, during the night of the great storm, a massive tree crashed in the woods behind. Its roots were wrenched from the ground, turning upward to explore the novelty of light, as it lay across the cinder track, blocking the way. I remember how I felt on seeing it; scorched and white, struck as the electric storm had raged around it and lifeless from the bolt. I should have been relieved that no one was killed but I felt wretched. I was overwhelmed by sadness which surprised me.

I knew that the tree could not continue to lie where it had fallen; soon men would come from the village and the air would hum with the noise of their saws. Soon the tree would be gone. Each day I returned like one hypnotized to watch from a distance as the work progressed. I witnessed the chopping, the cutting with cruel axe and the ruthless sawing. I stood silent as the final truck load was driven away. All that remained was a single root, its shaft so deep that none could shift it.

I ran all the way back to get my camera, dreading that in this time even the root would rot away and there would be nothing left to mark the tree's existence. I was breathless as I photographed it, not allowing myself time to recover from the run. I took wild, urgent frames, surrounding it from every angle. I knew in time there would be nothing left except the gap between some trees. But even their broken branches would mend. I photographed the gap. Each month it shrank, each month the space between became less obvious. Moss grew inside the hollow, carved out by absence. In spring this year it was a slight depression covered in primroses, and those heady bluebells which annually swamp the wood, making my eyes ache with colour. Now long grasses and briar wrap themselves around the sole root. When I take my daily walk it is the marker which tells me where I am and how far I have gone. It is the tree's memory.

I kept a record. I keep these exposures with others in a file marked 'Disappearance'. It is a file packed with the images of non-existence, like yesterday's reflections in a mirror. My images are shadows, memory, the half-forgotten kiss of a lover long gone, the impression of a child's small hand, fingers spread once upon a window pane.

Lately, I find that I cannot bear to exhibit much. The gallery agent tears his hair. He has clients. This is business. He tells me that I must understand his position. But he does not understand mine. Such work ought not to be fixed with a viewer's hard stare. Only shadows and memory, fading.

I never read reviews; a good habit of mine, like a daily walk. The reviewers have forgotten me, but not the paths I tread upon. They remember the impression of my feet, holding in muddy wetness the mark of size four boots days after I have passed. Soil remembers.

I have always been a solitary walker, going off on my own even as a child. Near the village where I grew up there was a route I walked habitually and although I have not been back for years, I could still describe it perfectly, which of course will not be how it is. I still see it as it was on the day everything changed; the day when everything moved into a faster, harsher age, and dragged me with it.

Known as the Mountain Road, it was reached by walking past the last straggling houses as they tailed away from the village, over the pavement which cut along the side of the RUC station. Now protective barriers isolate the building, but that kerb's placing long ago, meant that the station was always technically outside, because it was beyond the last street. This village was a place long used to settling its own affairs. Law was regularly taken into someone's hands; whether it was an argument about cattle or where somebody had placed a fence, the villagers dealt with it themselves. The chief cause of argument was land and grazing rights.

Mountain Road was not a proper road, but an untamed track which cars did not attempt. At the bottom it presented a false view of itself because some flagstones had once been laid, but the scheme for improvement was abandoned and they petered out behind the first turn. Out of sight from the village, the mountain took over as the track bent back into its wild nature. Nothing but brambles and hedgerow, no cheating pavement. Through the brambles on the right, the flat fields which dropped away from the mountain's side could be seen. These opened into yellow pasture which folded down into the coast. Here and there the odd barn stood darkly against the sky, but no one lived along Mountain Road.

There were two buildings which had stood vacant for as long as the oldest man in the village remembered. A

31

quarter of an hour's walk would bring me out by the first, which was a row of ruined dwellings where hay was stored. There were three compartments in the row, each with a half door and a tiny window that was sightless and black, probably always had been; light was a stranger, unable to illuminate those dark hours spent in a space no bigger than a bay for a horse. These had once been the homes of labourers who farmed the estate.

Facing them was the wood, a part of it which belonged to the estate, for the Mountain Road looped through its rigid ownership leaving an isolated and pathetic field on the other side, held in with barbed wire and a warning to trespassers. But the estate was bursting through its perimeters, a tangle of weed and briar which replaced the rusted fences that no one came to fix.

The estate occupied all to the left side of the track, apart from that one deviation, but it was held in by a crumbling stone wall that no one paid much heed to. Dogs ran in and out, and we were accustomed to take short cuts through the private land. The family who owned it had never lived there and the large white-stoned house was in decay. Sometimes we would see the estate manager walking in the grounds carrying a gun. But it was a silent stretch of land that was outside our experience, unlike the woods or the coastal path.

Further up the track was the other building, a cottage that bordered on to the back of the estate. This had never been let out to labourers and had no connection with the private land, yet it touched its outer wall in defiance. Its thatch was full of bird life and ivy, which had taken such a hold that the cottage was in danger of being transmuted into the mountain.

Then one day with no announcement, someone bought it. We only knew because carpenters and builders in the village received queries for estimates on repairs for the unnamed client.

Gradually from the ruined thatch, neat rows of red tiles

appeared. Window frames were put back in and painted bright green, and the client, an elderly white-haired stranger, moved in unceremoniously.

On my walks I now saw soft peat smoke from the once ruined chimney. We waited for the man to present himself to us. But we waited in vain, for by all accounts he was a cussed awkward character. He did not come down into the village, not even to attend mass, and he had his provisions delivered by Finnegans. The driver and delivery boy became the only ones to see him.

If I walked past when he was outdoors, he always managed to be at the back of the house by the time I drew close, warned by the sound of approaching footsteps. They said he was a recluse. I did not understand then.

We all admired him for taming that wild place; for reclaiming enough land out of the mountain to grow vegetables, clearing away impossible growth to plant neat rows of flowers. He kept a couple of goats, and Finnegans said that he milked them. But we knew nothing about him, apart from that, and we only learned his name through the grocer's list. Workers on the back fields said that they saw him leave his house once a fortnight. He would stand along the coast road to pick up the Ulster bus going into Belfast. Sean the driver told us that he went in to collect his pension, and that he was always back on the 5.15. His habits were regular and if he was solitary, he was certainly resourceful. The house was so well cared for, standing like a single defiant fist along that road, that we did not worry about him. Then stories began to reach us.

Finnegans went up one week to find the door bolted. The top half, which was usually left open, was drawn tightly shut. They noticed how odd the old man was becoming, the longer he stayed up there alone. He used to come out to settle his bill. Gradually this method of payment gave way to a brown envelope pinned to the gatepost in which the old man left money, and to which Finnegans sent the accounts. Once-weekly contact became too much for him. Sean the driver told us that he had missed his fortnightly trip. People wondered. Finally the local RUC went up. They discovered that the old man had family in Belfast who were in regular contact with him, and that was how it was left. He did not trouble us and we did not trouble him.

His cottage became one of my personal landmarks. As I climbed the steep side of the mountain walk I would get satisfaction from seeing it. The paintwork always looked fresh and the old man put bowls of flowers in the small windows. The half door was painted the same rich green as the window frames and kept open at the top so that a large gilt mirror, which hung behind, threw back the reflection of anyone passing. I wondered if it was intentional to return the curious stares of walkers?

As I reached the bend in the road on that particular day I knew something was wrong. There was a smell. That is what I always remember, for it was the first thing I sensed, that sickly smell of something turning sour. Decay. The air suddenly felt heavy, ready to rain and close in on me. Then I looked up.

Behind the border of grinning marigolds the cottage had been devastated. Every window in the front had been broken. The lower door was swinging open and I walked towards it, terrified of what I might find but compelled to look for it. I screamed, seeing a face that had been reassembled spin in front of me, distorted and crazy. The mirror had been shattered and my face reflected in its broken pieces as the cracks spread out from the centre. It seemed as though a weight, a hammer or a rock had been hurled at it, for the break was deliberate. There was no feeling of accident but an awful sense of premeditation.

I stepped over the shards of mirror guarding the open doorway like bright knives. Inside the building I shouted stupidly for help. Of course no one would come. I stood rooted. I could see through the cottage, all the doors were open. Everything had gone except a big iron bedstead which stood on its side against a wall. The mesh from its underframe scattered diamond shapes across the floorboards. Every piece of glass had been shattered, even the glass in the picture frame, hanging tenaciously in the small alcove next to the fireplace. And all over the floor were strewn bits of paper, torn up fragments with writing. I picked up a handful but could make no sense of anything.

There was a frightful smell of gas. It shocked me. I looked around. Some furniture had been piled up in one room. It looked as though two different sets of hands had been at work. One smashing everything, the other trying to impose order and sort through the wreckage. Someone had dragged the mattress out into the back garden. It was rain-sodden and rotten. I walked out to the back, compelled by curiosity. The rain barrel overflowed and already the down spout had caused a great damp patch to bruise the outer wall.

As I passed through what once served the man as a kitchen, I saw smashed bits of crockery everywhere, broken plates and splinters of china. Nothing which could be pieced together. I shudder still, remembering the sheer strength of the hand which had created so much energy to destroy what it had made. Because it was clear to me then that it was the old man who had done this. Nothing has ever changed my opinion on that, and nothing was ever discovered later to make me disbelieve my child's assumptions. A hand, driven with desperation and loneliness, finally giving back to the solitude what it asked.

I knew that it must have been gas. I could smell it, as though a canister had burst. I knew that those windows had been smashed in desperation to suck in air, and as life poured back so did rage at not being able to end it cleanly. I wondered whether the old man was alive or dead. Seeing the calmer hand which had imposed some order again, I told myself that his family had been here. In my mind I explained it all away to myself. But years later the image of that house was to recur to me, as I would puzzle the unexplained mystery. No one ever found out. The man vanished without trace. The house was once again unlived in. Mountain Road had triumphed.

On that afternoon I stood in the back garden sniffing the air. My young curiosity caught the smell of decay. It had been the first thing to warn me as I approached the house, and there it was again. I followed it down the garden and stopped short just as I almost stepped on the body of a fox, the cause of that smell. I knelt down to see it better. It was exquisite and dead. It lay on its side as if stretching, while the traces of putrefaction darkened its belly. Its bright, foxy eyes glistened, and its delicate head looked alert, as though it might yet sniff and walk cautiously away. Its brush was perfect although some of its underparts had burst. I bent over it and carefully touched the white tip of its tail and I seemed to realize what I hardly understand now; I saw that that was as close as I would ever get to a wild creature. Only through its death. As I thought that, a sickly feeling that was new to me turned in my own belly.

Later that evening I was to discover the brownish stains in my drawers that signified my womanhood. All at odds with my lanky thirteen-year-old child's body, yet I was expected to deal with it like an adult. I wanted to cry with my shivering sickness, but my mother was hard and cold.

'It's woman's lot so you'd better get bloody used to it.'

Her voice was devoid of any kindness. I was no longer a child whom she would comfort, but a symbol of time passing, and she was angry at my fertility which brought closer the end of her own. Her movements were brusque; she brought cotton wool, gauze, and two gold safety pins, and showed me how to fix it up. I was awkward and she was impatient with embarrassment.

When my father came home he carried the paper as usual but this night he waved it in the air like a flag. I knew already that I must not speak to him of what had happened to me because it was shameful, and not to be talked about with men. That night a silence grew up between myself and my father which never lifted. I was no longer his girl, I was destined to be some other man's woman. That was what my mother told me; one day I would marry and all this was necessary.

'You can't run about. Sit still. Don't be climbing or swimming or moving too quickly.'

I was immobilized through this strange time. All my wildness subdued.

My father was pale and troubled.

'Don't you ever look at a paper?' he snapped at my mother. 'You're bloody stupid, you are – you're totally unaware of anything. Look at this!'

He thrust the newspaper at her. She stepped back in case he would hit her but on this occasion the fight had left him. He went upstairs. I heard the bedroom door slam.

She sat at the table. She knew that she had been lucky, another night he might have swiped her good and hard. I used to lie upstairs and listen to her screaming and to his voice shouting, then the sound of blows and furniture being knocked over. Once a window smashed when he took her head between his hands and pushed it through the glass. His hands were cut to ribbons and she sat up half the night dressing his wounds, picking glass splinters out carefully. She was grazed on one cheek, but she was calm. That was how I always knew when the fights were over. The sudden silence as violent as the first shout, and my mother would sit tamely asking his pardon.

I kept thinking, as I watched her reading the headlines slowly, how I had touched a wild animal who had crawled into a garden for protection but was unable to leave, so the garden killed it. I watched my mother's motionless back over the paper, her arm moving clumsily as she traced the words.

I saw those headlines. Wilson was about to send the troops in to us. I had no idea how it would affect us. Would they come to our village?

*

The RUC station stands in a cage now. But don't be misled into thinking those of us on the outside are any more free.

The old man was on the outside and it drove him to despair. His departure from that place terrified me then, and each year it grows in significance. I said previously that I am a loner who is frightened of being alone. Each day I want to withdraw further from the world. Sometimes I even imagine that I am that old man. I dreamt recently about that mirror. The face I looked at was his, his as I imagined him because, you know, I never saw him. That dream terrifies me. I shake it off.

My family moved soon after that. We never went back, not even for a holiday. My father said it was a good place to have a funeral in, although we did not have his there either.

I work each day photographing things as they change, rot, and decay, knowing that I have time yet to reach into that old man's existence. Knowing that I still have time to record work for my file, and to plan my final piece of work which will be my ultimate statement as it will be my final act. Then I will have fulfilled the only true meaning of disappearance.

Bleeding Sinners

At level 9 of the Royal Victoria Hospital, the two women sat facing each other in the small waiting area for Clinic 9b. They smiled weakly, polite women, each wondering what the other was suffering from. They had both come in together and registered with the appointments clerk at the desk, but neither had caught the other's name. The seating space was small, the chairs put out in rows like a bus. A handful of women sat waiting already. The two newcomers studied each other, thinking that neither looked particularly ill. They thought that they were about the same age. They watched each other with curiosity while pretending to read the magazines, which had been left on a small table against one of the walls. On three sides were windows with dusty, grey venetian blinds that were closed. Outside the view would have been depressing: Cavehill, the Falls Road, the Divis flats and the maternity wing.

Eithne could not get her bearings, but she knew what was out there. She felt her stomach muscles contract, she was always nervous in the city. She had virtually stopped coming in since the troubles started six years ago. She wondered if the other woman was local. She would have liked to ask her how she managed, whether she was frightened. She did not look as if she was. She looked like the kind of woman who was scared of nothing, hard work or bullets.

The other woman was frightened. She was scared of hospitals. She wondered if anyone else was in for their six-weekly check-up. As she carefully glanced around, she noticed the greying hair and the attempts to conceal it, which on some became harsh blue-black against over-light complexions, on others the colour of brass. Maybe they had all had hysterectomies, maybe this was hysterectomy day when all the regional women were called in. She wondered if any of the others were from the country like herself. She was a farmer's wife.

She picked up *Practical Gardening* and half-heartedly turned the pages, looking at photos of hardy annuals. She should have been in Canada. The idea came into her mind and would give her no rest as she sat waiting for her name to be called. Canada. After all these years it still made her angry.

They had been newly married and ready to go, but his mother did so much crying that he didn't have the strength to leave. The 'aul country' called and he lost the will to tear up his roots. It was only for him that she stayed. Nothing else kept her here. A farmer's wife tied to the land, but she did not care for it. Unlike him. He was out every day, tramping the fields, putting down a scent like an old tom cat, while she had been cheated. Her own mother had been dying then, but she had given them her blessing and told them to go. Canada. What life was there for them if they stayed? But they remained behind. His mother saw to that. He was the youngest son, inheriting nothing. Evelyn tried to plead with him but he would not shift.

'And what sort of a son might I be, to go and leave my mother broken-hearted?'

Evelyn never forgave her mother-in-law. But he was a good man and she was a farmer's wife.

Eithne had picked up *Ideal Home* as she took a seat. She flicked through its pages. Room after room of muted pastel colours, of matching curtains and contrasting wallpaper: it looked all wrong. Didn't these people leave things out on tables like ordinary folk? Where did they pile their washing? Where did they leave their boots after a day's work? Eithne laughed, because she was a labourer's wife and could imagine the state of her kitchen after the kids and Joe had been through it once. Not that her life could have been any other way after all these years.

They had wanted to go to America but they never seemed to get the fare together. There were always more urgent things to spend money on, and then the babies started arriving. They should have gone out fresh, that first year they were married, but they let the time slide until it became nothing more than a fantasy; their life in America. Nothing held them here, neither security of job, nor of property. You rented yourself out as labour and you rented the house you lived in. Nothing was yours except the kids. He wanted to go on ahead and then send for her, but she would not consider it. She knew too many stories where men never came back, married to American wives. She had the children to think about. She did not want them growing up with a long-distance father; even if he did send money home, that wasn't what she had married him for. She was a labourer's wife.

The other woman watched Eithne out of the corner of her eyes. There was something sympathetic about her. She looked as though she might be married to a farmer, the kind of woman who would go to the ends of the earth with her man, like herself. Evelyn would have gone anywhere with her husband, especially Canada. And for him she ended up stuck in Ulster.

She felt at odds with everything here. She hated the people, but he wasn't like them. Even as a boy he'd been different. He would hold back and do things alone, rather than be dragged into a scheme he did not need. That was something she knew; when his mind was made up, he played stubborn, and there was no point arguing.

'I'll not put myself in with their union,' he said to her. 'I'll have no part with their orange politics. It makes no difference to me what religion a man is. If he's a farmer I'll judge him by his yeild, I'll not cut him in the market.'

She got to be the same. The neighbours criticized her for employing a Catholic man to lay floor tiles.

'He's an aul papist.' Ollie Ross's wife nudged her one day as if she was telling her a secret.

'Aye,' she answered, 'and he works damn hard too!' and she flounced past leaving her to say what she liked.

Evelyn had no time for their stupid quarrels. She was no more than seven or eight when she saw such hatred first-hand. She almost smelt it, as overpowering as the stench of paraffin. That's what they used when they burnt her family out. Her own people, solid Protestants, farmers like her father, yet they hurled storm lamps through their windows. She remembered the first sounds of breaking glass as a brick landed in the kitchen. Her mother came running from the scullery, drying her hands on her apron and screaming at them to get under the table and stay there. Evelyn squatted with Pauly, terrified, listening to noises outside: shouts and taunts, men's voices, and inside her father slamming the shutters of the kitchen windows. He wedged the largest tight with the broom handle.

'Get away from that window,' he yelled to his wife, who stood trying to pull heavy shutters together. They were too high for her. She was shaking, her movements slow and inefficient as she stood in the open frame of the glass, stretching up for the top. The bottom half of the window was unprotected and she stood; a slight, trembling woman, reaching up to make an arc against the navy-blue night, with the bright gaslight burning yellow behind her, like a flag to those in the dark fields.

'Get away from that window!'

He kicked the shutters together, and at the same time

heard the glass break as the stone crashed against it. The ones outside had waited until her mother was out of sight. They were neighbours of a sort.

Evelyn and Pauly watched the grown-ups. Their brother Henry was seventeen then, practically a man, while Jamsie, the eldest and cause of it all, was out at a dance. From her eight-year-old position she watched the adult feet running, and heard breaking glass as another window went through. Then there was a terrible stillness and a silence. Henry and her parents were whispering. Outside, the men were absorbed, soaking rags in paraffin. They pushed these oily rags between the smashed glass, up against the tight shutters. They pushed more sodden rags through the letter box, and tucked them under the wooden door at the back of the house. There was a loud crash, and a glow.

'The parlour window!' their mother screamed as their father charged into the next room. Inside, the curtains were blazing and the carpet already had started to melt. The sofa was turning into a misshapen hulk before his horrified eyes, and on the floor were three burning storm lamps, their glass shattered.

'We've got to get out or we'll be burnt alive.' He slammed the door on the fire to keep it back, but already the walls grew hot as inside the room melted. They were sealed in next to it.

Evelyn could not remember clearly what happened; she was dragged howling from under the table and carried roughly outside. Her father was standing in front of them with a shotgun, pointed at the night. Outside it was cool and her hair was damp on her forehead. Did she dream it, or had she seen the men with blackened faces running in all directions, as they scattered like wood-lice from an upturned stone?

'Taig lover!' The flat countryside rang with accusation.

'Taig lover!' Away into the darkening distance.

Evelyn never felt right about Jamsie after. He emigrated so she never did feel differently because she never got to know him. They said he was an idealist. He thought that he could change the world, but first he had to change the way people thought.

Standing for parliament indeed!

He thought that he could get on as a Progressive Unionist and push for things slowly. Well, she was eight, and she had been stoned as she walked in through the school gates. The children stood in a line along the wall and hurled them at her. She kept walking.

'Taig lover!' they shouted.

She was sent home at last, with a note for her mother explaining the difficulties. They had to consider the majority, and as the other children were told by their parents not to enter the classroom with the child whose brother stood for Progressive Unionist, they had no choice.

'Consider the majority!' her mother shouted. 'Pander to them if you ask me! The big farmers with the money. That's what they're talking about!'

Evelyn had been sent to another school way up in the city, and throughout that first winter her parents worried about her travelling all that way in the dark. She had not wanted to go at first, but she knew that she would never set foot in the old place. Even if they had a change of heart and asked her to come back, she would never walk through those gates. After her, none of her family went to that school again. It broke a tradition that her great-grand-parents had started. Something at least had changed, and by the age of eight she understood that ties of family and kin ought not to keep you. It was her own cousins who had stood in line, chanting with the rest. She wanted no ties of blood after that.

Then Jamsie left. Once word got round, he knew that he would never work again in that province. So much for ideals; he threw them all in and went to South Africa.

'You have to make the best for yourself,' he told them. She wanted nothing of their politics, not his, not anyone's.

She glanced at the forgotten magazine lying in her lap.

An advert caught her eye, offering lilies, boxed and delivered. She'd have to check whether they were white or orange before she could safely plant them in the boxes. She could always mix them, and leave them round the back. She had always liked lilies, and irises. She thought they were dignified flowers. She loved the shape of the petals, like little trumpets blowing with pride, but she could imagine if she had the orange type around the back. What would she say when Ollie Ross asked her if they were ready for the twelfth? She would have to order delphiniums.

Eithne was not reading *Ideal Home* any more. She was daydreaming, thinking how lucky they had been with their housing. They had lived with her parents and then with his elder brother. When they got the offer of the council house, they were overjoyed. At last something was being done for them. Modern buildings sprang up in their village against the historic skyline. They thought it was wonderful. They had four kids then and so they went up the list quickly. Lots of villagers put their names down for council properties, sick and tired of leaking, draughty cottages. Ten years later they saw how the modern buildings subsided, and the roofs leaked, and the doors had never fitted, saw how they had been turned into square boxes against the background of history that would outlast them as the new prematurely decayed, leaving them in their much waited-for slums. The history was being sold piecemeal to the new affluence which came out from the town. The old community were turning into the disadvantaged in their own village. She did not understand how it had happened. And all the while he was doing any job he could lay his hands on.

He was nimble-fingered, thank God. All he possessed was the skill at his fingertips. He picked up things here and there. How to lay bricks, set tiles, fix pipes, take out floor boards. And he worked for whoever asked him, aye, and paid him. He was not one who had to see a fellow's colours before he'd take on the job. Hunger felt the same regardless.

Evelyn knew that, too, as she looked at the pictures in the magazine. Orange lilies kept dancing in front of her, mocking her with their lascivious stamens. When he told her that time that he would join no orange union she had panicked, fearing the worst, and wondering what trouble there might be. But she was his wife, she went along with him. She would support any decision he made and if he would not ride the goat around the orange hall, then that was fine by her.

It was awful being young and first married. They had lived with his parents and she had never got on with her mother-in-law. Finally they bought the farm with a loan and spent the rest of their lives paying it back. But what else could they do? And then she was pregnant and had three, one after the other, and he looked at her that third time with her big swollen belly, laid out waiting for the midwife to arrive, and he'd promised her that it would be the last.

'There'll be no more, I swear it, I can't do this to you again.'

The birth had been awful. He stood outside the room horrified. It was his fault that his wife was being tortured, that's what he'd said to everyone after. She tried to tell him everything was all right, she did not blame him, but he wouldn't have it any other way.

'Not unless you want another,' he said, 'but only if you do, because I'll not put you through it again on my account.'

Eithne knew what it was to go through it again and again. Her husband was a fair man, he would take what work he could, he was not bigoted and he was cautious. She only wished he had been more cautious with her. Seven babies in nine years was a bit steep. She'd ask him to leave her alone and he'd look hurt as if it was him she didn't want.

'I want an end to all this,' she said, looking past him to the piles of nappies and unwashed clothes.

He was not stupid about work. He would pick and choose it. He would not take chances and go into dangerous areas. When the van came early to take them to a new site, the foreman would tell them where it was and sometimes no one stepped forward.

'You'll be all right as long as you don't open your mouths,' the foreman urged them. 'Come on, there's good money to be earned and you're wasting daylight.'

But how long could a man work without asking the time, or saying something, and the other workers would know. They looked different anyway. She could always tell. Stood out a mile. Not even able to sing on the way back in case anyone heard them in the van: 'And it's on the twelfth I love to burn the sash my father wore.'

But he went out to Protestant farms and fixed their roofs for them, and did as good a job as he would anywhere. He was fair. Although, God knew, she did the lion's share with babies. And you worried over your kids too, it wasn't as if once they grew up a bit you could relax. In fact she thought it was harder as they grew older. There were more things that could go wrong. Like the night the school bus did not come back.

It was November, dark by 5 pm. The bus was overdue; already it was half an hour late when one of her neighbours, whose son travelled on it, called round wanting to know what could have happened. Eithne did not think of it. In her mind she believed that a tyre had burst, something of that nature.

Around the square a group of anxious parents was waiting. Eithne put her coat on and went to join them. Someone had already phoned Malachy's and been told that the bus had left at the usual time. A couple of fathers decided that they would take a car and go over the route;

others wanted to go to the RUC. Eithne went back home. No point hanging about, they told each other.

Joe was working late. She sat tensely, dreading the knock on the door. When it came it was another neighbour, running, not able to stop.

'The station said that a bus has been hijacked, driven off the road. The driver's been taken. What in the name of God do they want with schoolkids!'

But the schoolchildren were turning up. Parents went out with cars and picked up as many as they could, and groups of them arrived in on their own.

Eithne was trembling. Joe still not home and she couldn't go out and leave the little ones.

'We've driven all around that point and still no sight of them.'

When her daughter at last walked in, Eithne thought she might faint. She and a friend had walked together, too scared to wait for the first cars. They walked home in the dark across fields. They had got lost and gone in a circle until they saw the road. It took them over an hour. She came in soaking. She had wet herself in fright. The urine smelt and Eithne saw her bare, frozen legs were mottled, and the skirt clung to them.

The bus had been forced off the road by armed men, their faces hidden by balaclavas. The driver was dragged from his seat and taken away. One of the men had walked up and down between the aisles, asking where the young men were.

There were four sixth-form boys on the bus, but the girls made them crouch under the seats and sat over them, terrified of what might happen if they were discovered. The man sneered at the children in their school uniforms, some not even eleven years old.

'Come on out of there, they're all culchies,' a man shouted to him from the road. Their accents were Belfast. The man paid no heed, continuing to walk slowly between the rows of terrified children.

48

'Any of you rabbit's litter get up to throwing stones?' he shouted, towering over them.

'Ah come out for fuck's sake. We've got the man we want, come on, they're only kids,' another called to him.

The girl told Eithne that her Sacred Heart Convent badge seemed to grow larger and stand out on her blazer.

They were all from Catholic schools up in the city. They were the ones who had passed the scholarships and had to be bussed in and out from the country. Rabbit's litter.

The driver had been forced into a field. They pistol whipped him. It was on the news. Her daughter's face was white. There were no heroics. No one thought they had been lucky to escape.

'Mam,' her daughter said, 'I pissed myself. That man said we smelt.'

Her daughter was ashamed.

They let the driver go with a warning. 'Take another route from now on. Next time you might not be so lucky.'

For a fortnight they had a police escort. When it was withdrawn, the driver went another way.

Eithne spent all that winter worrying about her daughter getting home safely. What could any of the parents do? There were no Catholic schools nearby that they could send their children to. There was one secondary modern, but it was full and would not take on a sudden influx of new pupils.

If that wasn't enough worry, around that same time her menstruation went wild. It was after the last child, her periods seemed to last longer and get heavier. It was as if something in her body had snapped; she had no energy and could not get through the day. Her younger sister came out to stay with them, during the worst times, to help. She did not know how she would have got through without her.

She hated her periods then. She had never seen so much blood. It used to frighten her. It spurted everywhere.

'I'm not just wearing sanitary towels but the big ones

49

from the bathroom at night,' she told her sister, who thought that she was joking. But it was no joke. The mattress got ruined and they had to pay for a new one. All this business people told her about lying down did not help. Blood still flowed.

'I could stand on my head and it would make no difference.'

She had to cover the bathroom in plastic sheeting every time she needed to change, or stand in the bath and hose it down after she had finished. It was a flood. No wonder she always felt tired. She would not go out the front door on those days, her sister had to pick the little ones up from school. If she went as far as the end of the street she'd be saturated. Her insides must have been coming away. And she did not get pregnant. That was what she could not understand. She lost four days out of every month being housebound. She stopped the doctor in the street one day and told him about it. He told her to go along to his surgery and he had a look at her.

'Good God!' His hands pressed the top of her stomach. 'You might be four months pregnant or you've something growing.'

She had to go to hospital to be scanned and wouldn't you know it, she was pregnant again, but the baby wasn't all that was growing; she had fibroids the size of golf balls.

They would not do anything for a year after the baby was born, a girl, waiting for the womb to shrink back to its original position. Then there was the waiting list, and for that year she had it on her mind that she had cancer. They told her that it would be unlikely that she'd ever conceive again.

'Jesus, Mary and Joseph!' she thought. 'About time!'

Evelyn was not bothered about having more children; she agreed with him that three were enough and their hands were full. He was a kind man, if it wasn't for him she would have been well out of it. Still, no matter where they had ended up living she would have had the same problems. Blood knew no social divisions, and she would have bled as much in Canada. She used to be plagued with her periods. They became heavy after the second birth. She would wear five sanitary towels together and still seep through. There was so much blood she could not get to the end of the lane, but would turn back soaking. She would not go into anyone's house because everyone would smell blood. Though, God knows, you could smell a whole lot worse things out in the country. She had heard women calling others hussies, because they let their men know. It was shocking.

Evelyn remembered her aunt once telling her about some woman who had walked past her husband with a packet of towels under her arm. 'Imagine carrying on like that, as bold as brass!'

In all her married life, her aunt never once let her husband find evidence. 'They would go right off you if they ever found out the half of it!' she said, wrinkling her nose in disgust. 'I've made sure that he hasn't been troubled by anything like that,' and she screwed her face up at the unpleasant memory.

Evelyn wondered what her aunt would think of her now, if she was still alive. She had no choice but to let her husband know, she bled so heavily it would have been impossible to hide the event. He always knew, he could tell by looking at her.

'I'll feed the chickens on my way in,' he'd say. 'Don't you be running about when you've got your period.' Straight out with it he used to come. She never let anyone know. 'It will do the chickens good to have to wait. Let them learn some discipline.'

And she had laughed with him at the idea of well-disciplined chickens. Maybe they would lay on demand.

'Aye, we'll be set up like the big farmers then, eh? Rows of chickens as far as the eye can see.'

But they were never set up like that.

Well, a lot worse things could happen. They were both still alive, and sometimes she could not take that for granted. Like the time that man broke in. She had been having one of her awful periods then. Porter was round at a neighbour's helping to deliver a calf. It was late; dark and wet outside, and the man broke in through a side window in the kitchen, the one she left slightly open for the cats. It gave her such a shock; a tall man dripping in the kitchen. She could not understand why he had not knocked. Then she realized, and at the same time saw who it was. She knew him, a local farmer. And she could smell his breath from where she stood.

'What do you want?' she asked him.

His voice was coarse, she could hear it still. The way he spat the words, telling her that he had come to show her what a real Ulsterman could do, unlike the one she was married to, who had no decent blood in his veins. She shuddered at the memory; her husband was bloodless because he would join no Protestant union. That man had come to warn him; either to join up or get out, and the way he thought to do it was by frightening her. She had been disgusted at the cowardly tactics more than anything. She never told her husband. He would have worried, and probably joined up to stop her being harmed. If they wanted to threaten him they could do it to his face, she would not be intimidated for them both.

'Who put you up to this?' she asked.

He took a step forward, but she was too quick for him because he had been drinking. She caught him with her knee. She wanted to paralyse him. Make sure he fathered no more. He doubled up. She took the gun down from behind the door. All it had in it were the pellets Porter used for shooting mice, but she made as if to fire it and elbowed him into a wooden chair. He slumped across the kitchen table.

'Don't move!' she warned. 'Or so help me God, I'll fire,

and the chances are I'll kill you because I'll not fire to wound, but straight to your head. I don't want to miss.'

The man looked up through bleary eyes. 'You're the one that went to the other school, we weren't good enough for you, were we? You and your fancy brother with his new-fangled ideas.'

He hated her. While her back grew rigid and her desperation made her strong, he feared her too.

She told him to keep quiet. 'I'll discuss nothing with you.'

That was it, the old grudge for something that she was not responsible for. She was still being blamed.

Nauseous with contempt, she felt she would choke, but still she trained the gun at the man's head. Blood started to run down her legs. Who was the more disgusting now?

Her husband's old mac was hanging by the door. Slowly she edged over to it. The man dozed in his drunkenness, head down on the table. Still she would not drop the gun. She held it in one hand and put her arm through the sleeve, changing over without once pointing the barrel away from his head. He looked ill. His sweat stank, sour and poisonous. She hoped he would not die. Not that she cared whether he continued to live, but she did not want to have to explain how his corpse got into her kitchen.

'Please God,' she prayed, 'let him get up and walk away.'

But the man looked set for the night. He had forgotten her, as he had forgotten his mission. Belching, he turned his head to one side. His oily skin looked grey.

'Please God, don't let him throw up here.'

She found a piece of string in the mac's pocket, and tied it around her waist to keep the coat tight about her. It reached to the ground. She was still wearing wellingtons from mopping the tiles down. They felt cold on her feet. Even her perspiration started to freeze. She felt more blood run down her legs. It was warm, and now she did not care. For what felt like hours the man slept and she would not move away from him. His hand rubbed his nose. She stuck

53

the gun barrel against his face. He was confused and came out of his sleep roughly. Maybe he wanted it to be a dream, but she stuck the cold metal barrel into his cheek. His eyes were terrified now.

'Turn and go,' she ordered.

The man, white and ill, unable to stand erect, pulled himself up by the table. She stuck the gun in his shoulder blades, her arms beginning to shake violently with the strain of holding it out.

'Move!' she screamed.

He shuffled, head down. She pushed him with the gun. As long as it was between them, she could push. She could not have touched him.

He shambled through the back door and she followed, prodding with the shotgun's cruel metal tip, until he was on the drive.

'Keep walking.'

She cocked the trigger and stood pointing into the darkness, until the shadowy figure had disappeared along the main road. Slowly, she walked back to the house, but she did not go inside. She leant against the lime-washed wall, breathing heavily. Possibly she blacked out, because the next thing she was conscious of was the sound of his car as it pulled up the drive.

She ran in and threw the gun up on to a shelf. He came in immediately she had done this. She was sure he must have heard the gun clatter, but he only looked a little surprised. It was without suspicion that he asked her why she had his coat on. She muttered about the cold.

'The gun's out of its place.' He looked concerned. 'I'm sure I didn't leave it there, I always hang it up.'

She laughed stiffly. 'I was lookin' mice,' she said, and he laughed at the idea of her with his old mac on, hunting.

'God, the things you get up to when I'm not here,' he grinned.

'What did you deliver?' she said quickly. 'I mean, did the cow calve or have you left it?'

She did not know whether she was making sense or talking gibberish, but she kept looking at him.

'Oh aye,' he said, 'about half an hour ago. We had a drop to celebrate. I must get out of these things though.' He was bathed in sweat. 'It was a long hard birth. Bertie did most of the rope work, but even so, water was pourin' off me. We were sweatin' bullets the pair of us. And him – worried he'd have to send for the vet – when the hind legs just came free. One minute the calf was stuck and the next, it was standing up and the old cow was licking it clean. Bertie nearly collapsed.'

'Oh, that's nice,' she said.

He looked puzzled. 'Bertie collapsing?'

Then she looked down and noticed that her wellingtons were bloody.

'I'll run the bath for you,' she said, and went upstairs.

She took the boots off, holding them over the toilet bowl, but the blood was viscous. Most of it clung to her bare legs rather than the wellingtons. She swished water around in them and tipped it down the lavatory. Quickly, she put her legs under the taps of the bath and soaped furiously. She hid the boots in the hot press. She could sort them out later. Then she started to run the bath. It struck her that for the first time in their married life, she was keeping blood a secret from him. She went downstairs, hanging the coat up as she went.

'Your bath's running,' she shouted, as he stood rinsing his hands in the kitchen sink. 'I'd get up before it overflows.'

When they offered Eithne a hysterectomy she agreed immediately. 'Anything that gets me out of this mess,' she said, thinking about all the bloodstains that needed to be washed out every month.

They explained to her that it was as easy to take the whole thing out, at the same time as they removed the fibroids. After a long wait, events speeded up. She felt that she had only got over the shock of the letter, giving the date for the operation, when she was admitted; and it was done.

She made arrangements for the children to stay with her sister, but up to the minute she was wheeled into the theatre, she could not believe that it was happening. Only when she saw the doctor wearing wellingtons did it become real to her. The last thing she could remember was staring at the doctor's white wellingtons, and wondering if outside it was very wet.

When she came home she told Joe that she would be the shape of the armchair. 'It'll be as much work as I can do to lift a cup of tea.'

And all that last month she sat indoors, feeling weak. Joe did everything. The baby was only thirteen months old, but they decided it was best to send her to the sister's, for Eithne was just like a baby herself. She giggled, thinking how he had fussed. The kids had been great, although finally he sent the three youngest to stay at his mother's.

'They can't be creeping around the house quietly all the time,' he said. 'They're lively, high-spirited kids. They'll have to stay at Mam's until you can manage with a noisy house.'

It had been strange having her kids come to visit her, and her sitting in the armchair like royalty. Her sister brought the baby up every day and Eithne would sit with her, but Anne would not let her change her, or do any work. She was free to sit, cuddling her baby. It was lovely.

'You're my last,' she told the little one, as the realization grew on her. 'My last.'

The baby was so precious and for four special weeks she could enjoy her, in a way that had been denied with the others. A rare month of being cosseted, a rare month of playing with her daughter and knowing that when she was exhausted, she could hand her back to someone and her responsibility ended for the day; heaven.

Not that she wanted to prolong her convalescence. She

did not forget how shocked she was when she had tried to walk upstairs that first night, and had to be carried back to the living-room in a sweat. Even crossing the room tired her out.

'Mother of God! Is this the improvement they told me to expect?'

Joe made up a bed in the living-room, and her eldest daughter crept about quietly.

She lay there, wondering if they had cut away all her vitality along with her womb. Surely it would not affect her like this, if they had done it correctly? She began to imagine that they had made a mistake. She felt like a dead person sometimes. Suddenly depressed, then it would clear, and she would enjoy life, her baby, and feel good. It was a confusing time for her. But gradually she was gaining strength. Every day put her further along the way of recovery.

Her sister told her one day that she was looking wonderful. Eithne laughed, but after Anne had left, she looked at herself in the bathroom mirror, the upstairs being once again accessible to her. Her face was thinner, her eyes looked larger and darker.

'By God, but you're a good looking woman,' she told the mirror and smiled with genuine surprise.

It felt good. Energy was flooding back. No more periods, no more pregnancies. Freedom. She was lucky.

When they offered Evelyn a hysterectomy she did not want to have it done.

'I was born with my womb, and I've a good mind to die with it,' she told the doctor at the Royal who first suggested the operation.

'What do you want your womb for?' he asked. 'A lifetime of bleeding and being a prisoner in your own home? You told me that you didn't want any more children, you said it was decided years ago. You've had five curettes to date and there's been no improvement. Frankly,

57

I can suggest nothing else other than removal. You can sit it out, of course, and hope that the menopause will give you some relief from this cycle.' He did not sound hopeful.

'I'm forty-three, doctor . . . how long will I have to wait?'

'You could have had this done ten years ago, after you'd had all the children you wanted. It would have changed your life.'

Aye, she thought, and changed me too. God knows how I might have ended up, an empty shell with all my insides cut out. How would I even know I was still a woman, neutered like a cat? Some pathetic creature that went against its nature and they tell you not to let men know you bleed, because it will disgust them. Wait until they heard this one. She would keep quiet all right, so would he.

'All right,' she said. 'I'll have it done.'

They did not warn her that after she would feel so tired. She felt tearful much of the time and angry. She wanted to blame someone, but did not know who. The monotony, waiting to recover as she sat in a chair in the kitchen while he worked the land. He was not able to stop and spend time with her. She felt desperate for company, as if the operation had triggered off a need in her that would always be unfulfilled. She listened to the clock ticking, to the mice scratching, to the rare sound of a car passing. On delivery days she was animated, making tea for the drivers, keeping them late by talking, telling her life's history in one short morning. After that activity, she would collapse in a chair, sweating and sickly. He would find her slumped in the same place each evening.

He tried to get neighbours round to sit with her, but distance was always a problem. People never used to drop in on them with facility, and some of those neighbours had been responsible for publicly ostracizing him, for not going along with their union. He was the odd fellow, and so their wives were wary of getting over-friendly with the odd fellow's wife after they heard their husbands talking.

All three of her children now lived in England. Her two daughters came home for a week during the first stages, taking time off work, but they had to go back. She needed company, she needed the impossible. Day after day, she sat in a chair. She took no pleasure in anything, even when the girls were home, she seemed to use up the time quarrelling. She lost all incentive to do anything. She even stopped knitting, one thing she enjoyed.

'What's the point of knitting fancy cardigans, if you never go anywhere to be seen in them?'

One of the neighbours sent her some fine yarn with a card, hoping that she was better. It was a kind thought, but useless. The wool remained in skeins for weeks after; even winding it into balls was too much effort.

She looked around the waiting-room thinking that she should have brought the wool with her, at least she would have had something to do, instead of having to pretend to read the plant catalogue. She shut the magazine irritably. She hated coming into Belfast. She worried about him walking round the city. She hated the idea of it and her nerves were on edge. How was he spending the day?

He had driven in with her and put the car into the car park for three hours.

'You won't be longer than that surely?' he asked.

At first he was going to come and wait with her, but she told him to go and do something useful, he'd be fidgety all the time and it would drive her mad. He told her that he would drop in on Ainsworth's, the building suppliers in May Street. He had ordered cement from them and they had delivered the wrong type. When he phoned to make up the order, the girl he spoke to did not seem to know the difference between one sort of bond and another.

'I'll drop in while I'm up here. I can go through the catalogues in the shop and order over the counter. At least I'll be able to see what the clerk writes down, and I can check on the date for them to pick up the original delivery.

Then I'll just go for a dander about town. I'll get back for a quarter past two.'

She must have looked anxious because he changed it to half past.

'Is that OK?' he asked.

'Don't worry about me,' she told him. 'I'll just sit here. If you don't see me, you'll know I'm still in with the specialist. Just wait here until I get out.'

Evelyn stretched forward to put the magazine back on to the table and at the same instant Eithne did. Their hands just brushed each other's. They apologized before drawing into their chairs, straightening away from each other into the hard plastic seats.

'Sorry.'

'Sorry.'

This was their first check-up as out patients. They both glanced at their appointment cards: 1.15 and 1.30.

The clock on the wall was ticking past those times already. It stood at 1.40.

Eithne was not that bothered. She had arranged to meet Joe at the site. He was working in Belfast all week, putting in an extension to a builder's shop. He left early in the morning while it was still dark. She heard him moving around. He wrote out the address on a scrap of paper and left it for her on the kitchen table.

'Just come round to the site hut whenever you get finished and we can travel back on the bus together. I'll tell the foreman that you're coming, and say I want to get off work as soon as possible after you arrive. There won't be any problems.'

She hoped that there would not be. There were only a few buses a day to their village, so she had to pay attention, otherwise they might end up missing them and she would have to ride back in the works van. She did not fancy that. All the men being polite and awkward with a woman among them, a fellow's wife at that. God knows, they might ask her how she got on, if he'd told them she'd been up at the Royal. She would be all embarrassed sitting there.

She might feel different if it was her tonsils she'd had taken out, but not that.

Eithne glanced again at the clock: 1.45. She did not want to be too early meeting Joe. He'd only lose more pay.

Women shuffled their feet. She'd bet that plenty of them had been given the same appointment time as her. These doctors thought that they could see five people simultaneously. She felt the sudden change of mood as women looked up. The cause of it was a nurse who appeared carrying a clipboard. She looked towards the rows of seats.

'Mrs McGrattan?' she called as every woman looked at her expectantly. The one whose name was called stepped up, like a winner at bingo, and was ushered into a room off the corridor. The nurse called a second time. 'Mrs Shaw?'

Another woman was directed into the other examination room. Those remaining, which included both Eithne and Evelyn, sat back in their chairs.

The movement of all leaning forward by one or two inches brought with it an easing of tension, as if the entire group had been activated at the same moment. There was a twinge of solidarity and the first exchanges were made to break the silence.

'Did you travel a long way to get here?' someone asked, neither caring if they did or did not, but the questioner herself had, and wanted to tell the listener of the awful time she spent on the bus.

'No, I live locally,' replied the unwitting catalyst.

'Oh dear God, you won't know the half of it . . . .'

'Isn't the weather shocking?' others asked themselves, while others hoped that they would not be kept waiting all day.

'What time is your appointment? Oh God, so's mine. Isn't that sensible of them?'

'I'm in for fibroids. I don't know what's going to happen. They might keep me in after the check-up.'

'I told them they could do what they wanted. I told

them, I'm through suffering. I've had my Purgatory on earth.'

'Aye. Men don't know the half of it.'

'Oh Jesus, I'm widowed now . . .'

'Don't you think it's worse when you're on your own?'

'Don't be talking soft; . . . I wish to God the Lord would take mine from me now. He's that ill. He's a vegetable really. Mind you, he was when I married him, it's not a medical condition, if you know what I mean. I was young and soft; he had black hair, shiny with brilliantine; must have turned my head. I can't think what else it was.'

'I'd have mine back like a shot, but the Good Lord called him home. He was hit by a bit of falling masonry on the way back from work. I was a young widow. God's played me a cruel hand. But we never know the reason, do we? He's got some plan.'

Evelyn said nothing. She looked up and caught another woman's eye. Eithne smiled a little too formally, and both withdrew into silence. At the desk the receptionist switched on the radio and fiddled with the dials.

RADIO DOWNTOWN YOUR LOCAL RADIO STATION. FIRST WITH THE NEWS AND VIEWS AND THE BEST IN MUSIC. STAY TUNED.

'Oh God,' a woman groaned behind Eithne. 'I hate that soft feller, that you know, Freddy . . . whatsisname . . .'

'Oh, him, is it?' a woman said. 'Tell me, is it time for the phone-in programme? I usually like that.'

'Oh you don't, do you? You get some funny people ringing in. They talk all sorts of rubbish.'

'I know, that's why I like it. It makes me feel that there are others worse than me.'

'Well, I heard one the other week . . .'

Evelyn switched herself off like she would have the radio. It was only the phrase 'sins against nature' which drew her back. She overheard it and felt herself stiffen. She knew that it would be unwise to open her mouth now, but she continued to listen, drawn like a magnet, to that which might offend her most.

'And they have the cheek to say to you that you could have used something. Half the bloody doctors in this place are hell bent on murder. And you look them in the eye and say that you don't believe in altering God's plan, and by Jesus they can't look you straight.'

'It's terrible,' another voice said. 'Last time I was up here, this young one, bit of a kid he was, said to me, "After eight children it's not unlikely that you should have a prolapse," like it was me own bloody fault.'

'I said to one of them, "What did God give us wombs for if they weren't meant to be used?" and he couldn't answer me.'

'Jesus, I'm not surprised,' said another woman, whose voice was low, well controlled, and had been up till then as silent as Evelyn. 'It's the likes of yous is keeping this province back. It's the twentieth century not the middle ages.'

'You lot are out-breeding the decent Ulster folk,' another new voice spoke.

Evelyn felt her palms grow cold.

'Here, what do you mean, "you lot"?' said the voice that did not want to be held back in the middle ages. 'Just who are you calling "you lot"?'

The voice was harsh, not an ally to the surprised second speaker. 'For your information,' it continued, 'I'm a Catholic; but I'm progressive. I haven't out-bred anyone yet.'

'Ah, how can you call yourself progressive, if you believe in all that praying to statues and bloody holy virgins?'

'Oh, that's nice!' an older woman said. 'That's nice, isn't it? You want to mind your language.'

'I agree. I'm shocked.'

'Don't make me laugh. In the name of God . . .'

'Just you leave God out of this! You don't know what you're talking about.'

'I do! I know better than you. When did any of yous study a bible, hey? When have any of you lot actually read God's word, and I mean His word? Not the ravings of some demented priest on a Sunday. There isn't one of you Holy Marys could quote from the bible. No, you'd rather have it all Latin, and mumbo-jumbo that you don't understand, and you go round in your processions mouthing words.'

'At least we pray,' someone shouted. 'We don't go round waving flags, shouting about this battle and that battle.'

'Ah, the pope wears a frock!'

'My arse!'

'Oh, that's nice, isn't it, that's nice. Language! You don't have to lower yourself to their level.'

'Who's lowering themselves? Yous are like rabbits, the way you carry on.'

'I don't forget a face,' one of the older women said. 'I'll not forget ye . . . and on the day of judgement,' she lifted her head piously, 'on the day of judgement, I'll ask Our Lord to forgive you.'

'Don't you pray for my soul, I don't want any favours from you.'

'Look,' said the progressive voice, 'it doesn't have to be like this; we each have the right to live our lives the way we see fit – '

'It's a sin against God and nature,' said one of the older women. 'All this carrying on. No one can just do as they please. God is watching and He knows. It's filthy, all this business; none of us have the right to twist God's will. If He wants us to get children, He gives them to us in His mercy.'

'Oh, when did He last stick it up you then, love? Divine intervention was it? That's what they all say.'

'God strike you dead! Blasphemer!'

The oldest woman leapt to her feet clutching a newspaper, which she started to roll up. Another waved her handbag in the air in the direction of the progressive voice.

'I've never heard such filth!' the first woman said, as beside her another hunted in her bag for the bottle of holy water she would not come up to the city without. She started sprinkling this over the waiting women. As drops fell on them, a woman screamed as if she had been scalded.

'Keep your superstitious witchcraft off me!' she yelled, wiping her coat sleeve furiously.

A nurse stormed up, hat askew, fob watch flapping.

'Ladies! Ladies!' she shouted over the commotion until she had their attention. 'What is going on here? May I remind you that this is a hospital. There are seriously ill people in other parts of the building, who come in here for treatment expecting peace and quiet. Any more displays like this, and I shall be forced to request that certain parties go and wait elsewhere.'

Both Evelyn and Eithne sat stiffly through the exchange, although Eithne did turn around rather quickly to see who had accused them of breeding like rabbits. Otherwise they were both immobile. They were calm, controlled women. Evelyn knew that she was well out of their politics – look where it got people – and she was well out of their religion. She prided herself on that. She went to chapel when she felt the need; it was something personal, above bigotry.

Eithne for her part felt embarrassed. She did not agree about 'sins against God and nature', but on the other hand, she knew nothing to counteract the hard facts of life; no one had ever told her the ways of avoiding pregnancy. Her local doctor would have been scandalized by the suggestion, and the only talk she'd ever had about sex life was the one before she got married, where the priest had blushed and stammered about sins of the flesh. And Joe was as clueless. The younger ones today, even her daughters, all knew more about it than she ever would.

If they had gone to America it would have been different. A great big place like that, she ought to be able to find a doctor who would not know her. She could get a Jewish one, someone who would not ask, nor even care, if she was a Catholic.

Outside, she heard the sound of ambulance sirens as if they were racing in a pack the way dogs might run, three or four together, wailing alongside the others. Then she heard what sounded like a police car. It was in the distance, but slowly its sound picked up as it joined in the slow cry. She hated the sound they made, it always made her panic. She expected that the nurses got used to it, hearing them every day, but she felt that she never could.

WE INTERRUPT THIS PROGRAMME TO BRING YOU A NEWS FLASH.

The receptionist turned and all heads looked towards the desk where the radio sat. The newscaster continued in his calm, removed voice.

A BOMB EXPLODED NEAR THE CITY CENTRE AT APPROXIMATELY 1:30 THIS AFTERNOON. ALL STREETS AROUND DONEGALL SQUARE HAVE BEEN CLOSED TO TRAFFIC AND THE IMMEDIATE AREA OF MAY STREET HAS BEEN CORDONED OFF.

MOTORISTS TO EAST BELFAST ARE ADVISED TO USE THE ORMEAU ROAD AND TO AVOID THE ALBERT BRIDGE AREA, WHICH IS ALREADY VERY CONGESTED.

POLICE AND AMBULANCES ARE STANDING BY, BUT THE EXTENT OF THE DAMAGE IS DIFFICULT TO ASSESS. NO OFFICIAL FIGURES HAVE BEEN RELEASED YET.

There was a small silence and the newscaster continued:

A MAN WAS SHOT DEAD ON A BUILDING SITE EARLIER THIS AFTER-NOON. THE SITE, WHICH IS NEXT TO THE AINSWORTH CONTRACTORS, WHERE THE FULL DAMAGE OF THE BOMB BLAST OCCURED, HAS BEEN SEALED, SO THAT SECURITY FORCES MAY UNDERTAKE INVESTIGA-TIONS. SO FAR IT IS NOT KNOWN WHETHER THE TWO INCIDENTS ARE LINKED.

The radio crackled and buzzed, the receptionist twisted the dial until it cleared, and the sound was sharp.

THE RUC HAVE SET UP AN ENQUIRY DESK. RELATIVES AND FRIENDS CAN RING BELFAST 5000, 6000 AND 6200. I'LL GIVE YOU THOSE NUMBERS AGAIN ... AND IT'S JUST COME THROUGH THAT PEDES-TRIANS ARE BEING ALLOWED INTO THE AREA WHILE ALL TRAFFIC IS BEING TURNED BACK ....

'Hi!' said a voice, different, snappy. The voice of play, no longer the voice of reason.

'Hi!' this fresh voice said, drawing the listeners back from their vision of blood and trouble.

'Hi!' it shouted, calling the listeners into its frequency of youth and carefree days.

'Hi!' it screamed, for ignorance is bliss.

'Let's have a rave from the grave. A good old sixties number. This will take you back, those that can remember back, and I'm talking to the mums and dads now, yes, I'm talking to you. Remember it, fellers, when you couldn't work up the courage to ask that girl to dance? Do you ever ask yourself . . . where is she now? She could be listening in right at this moment!'

She could be lying on the ground with her brains blown out, thought Eithne as pop music came flooding back.

Evelyn sat trembling while the words played over in her head. THE FULL FORCE OF THE EXPLOSION OCCURED IN AINSWORTH'S.

Eithne's mind was reeling. With her brains blown out . . . like Joe, she thought. He was working in the centre. The site was next to a shop. He was building the extension. Ainsworth's. He had not told her the name. Suppose it was. She heard the words clearly as if the radio still talked about it. MAN SHOT DEAD ON BUILDING SITE.

Of course there was more than one building site in the city. But how many were next to shops? Jesus! Where had she put that piece of paper? She fumbled with shaking hands in her bag. Her breath was coming in gasps. She snatched the crumpled piece of paper and as she read it, she stood up, ashen-faced and terrible. Evelyn too had risen to her feet. The two women spoke under their breath, but it was with one voice, white-lipped and hating.

'The bastards!'

*

Outside, ambulance sirens became urgent as people realized where they were going.

'They'll be rushed off their feet in casualty,' the progressive voice said, turning to the rabbit neighbour, animosity forgotten.

'Well, they didn't say there were casualties, did they?' the rabbit replied.

'No, but they gave out the numbers, and they only do that when there's been people injured.'

'They could have evacuated the building in time, you never know.'

'Well, I think they'll be flat out, they might take some round to the City too. I'd hate to be a doctor.'

'Oh, God help us, so would I! But there's no chance of that,' she said comfortingly, as both sat back in their chairs to wait for their names to be called.

Eithne crossed to the receptionist. 'Let me use your phone,' she said.

'It's not for public calls, there's pay phones down stairs on the ground floor.'

'But my husband was there.' Eithne gasped for air unable to explain.

'I'm sorry?' the receptionist said. 'I don't understand you.'

'My husband!' Eithne screamed.

The receptionist looked disconcerted. She stared hard at the mad woman in front of her and began reasoning. 'I can see that you are extremely distressed . . .'

But Eithne cut across her, shouting that her husband was on the site that had been bombed. But the phone on the desk was for internal calls only. There was no outside extension.

'I'm sorry,' the receptionist said, her eyes shocked. 'But you will have to go downstairs . . . would you like someone to come with you? . . .'

Eithne was already speeding through the double doors. The lift was occupied so she ran down all flights.

*

Back on level 9, the nurse approached the woman who was standing like one hypnotized.

Evelyn did not see her. She did not hear her name being called, not the first nor the second, nor even the third time.

The nurse approached cautiously, the way she might a large dog that had slipped its leash and was terrorizing children. 'Mrs Irvine? That is your name?'

Evelyn stared at the nurse as if through a telescope held the wrong way round, making the woman small and odd. She peered. The nurse squirmed, but attempted a smile as she told the woman that the doctor was ready to see her now. The nurse hoped that any second the strange woman would snap out of her trance, say something about being in a world of her own and then they would both laugh, the awkward moment over. But the strange woman did no such thing. She stared past the nurse.

'Mrs Irvine, the doctor . . .'

'Stuff your bloody doctor!' the woman shouted. 'Stuff him!'

'Really, I know that you have been kept waiting this afternoon, but there's no need . . .'

The woman picked up her bag and walked past the nurse.

'I take it that you are cancelling your appointment?'

Evelyn did not reply.

'This will look very bad on your record you know . . .'

Evelyn kept walking.

'Well, could you at least sign this form, because it might be months before an appointment can be made? And there's the question of liability . . . if anything goes wrong . . .' The nurse pursued her out through the doors.

Evelyn turned on her heel.

'Piss off!' she spat as she started to run.

The nurse walked back to the gynaecology ward shaking her head. She was puzzled. First there had been that shameful episode when she had to go in and warn them about the noise; now this. You never could tell.

On level 2, the ground floor, Evelyn ran straight past the admissions clerk who sat back in her office, its slice of window open as a counter to the public. Two telephones were ringing at once. The clerk took one up and told whoever it was to wait, before picking up the next. Evelyn was out of the front of the hospital and on the Falls Road. She noticed everything. She wondered if she was in shock because she had a sense of heightened awareness, everything she saw deepened in significance, seemed to have some great meaning, if only she could understand what it was. Everything crashed on to her consciousness with crystal precision. As though long-sighted, she could discover things way beyond her in the distance. The clerk answered two phones in slow motion. Everything was precious. The next half hour would be a stage in her life when she would not know whether her husband was alive or dead, but there would be hope. After that half hour, she doubted what would remain.

Images danced in front of her vision. The graffiti on the brick wall outside the hospital were large and menacing. The armed cars cruising the Falls looked greener. The young soldiers pointed guns as the saracens progressed upwards.

Opposite, the white statue of the Virgin Mary mocked them all. Cold and icy, it stood in the private grounds of the school, unresponsive to the army as it was to life. That was the key to it all, Evelyn thought. She was alive, tasting the sharp edge of death with hot breath; death, which could present itself any time, and in one second or less, complete its mission. A bullet to the brain. Would you even feel it? Would you even know? It would happen so quickly that you alone would never realize you were dead. Brutal as that. After-life? She could not bear to think about it. If there was anything, she no longer cared.

She crossed the road. Facing her was a Catholic church. She had not noticed it when Porter drove her down. How could she ever have missed it? A nun came up from the side street, frog-marching a group of schoolgirls in maroon uniform. The tallest towered over the tiny figure in authority. It was windy. The nun's veil blew behind her; a black flag it flapped, heavy cotton serge. It made a noise that reminded Evelyn of damp sheets flapping on washing lines; too heavy with water to be blown in the breeze, they would hang straight down and make a sad grey sound, and drip into puddles on the grass.

She saw the life-size crucifixion in the church garden as she passed. Again the statues were white and shiny in freezing intensity. Bloody Catholics, she thought, they're in love with death, that's why they build their churches near hospitals, hoping that after the sacraments they can slip quietly over and die, their souls intact and purified.

She turned her back on the scene and made for the city. She cut through Grosvenor Road and found herself in Howard Street. Her heart felt as if it would explode. She was sure that everyone could hear it beating.

Eithne was still in the Royal. At the pay phone she fumbled for coins and waited her turn for the one phone which worked. She concentrated on taking control of her breathing. Tried to focus her mind. Impossible. There was one woman in front of her.

'Please,' Eithne said, 'please let me go on, I've just heard the news flash. I'm worried for my husband.'

'So am I love, so am I,' the woman replied.

'No, you don't understand. . . . ' Eithne tried to explain. 'My husband was working on the site where the man was shot . . . .'

'Look, my husband is supposed to pick me up, and with the traffic all over the place, God knows how he's going to get in. I have to talk to him before he leaves work because he's got to pick the kids up from school, and they'll be standing out on the street in this weather. . . I'm worried about my kids.'

'My husband could be dead,' said Eithne, starting to shake.

'Oh, Good God Almighty!' the woman stepped back, and as the phone became free she pushed Eithne forward. 'Go on dear, you call up.'

Eithne's hands shook so much that the woman had to dial for her. All three numbers were engaged. Eithne was in a rage with the hopelessness of it all. She stood not knowing what to do. Someone brought her a cup of tea, but she could not drink it. The ground floor of the hospital was being turned into a makeshift ward for people suffering from shock, as the first consignment of casualties arrived. Stretchers were carried through, and there was a lot of shouting. People were everywhere, as one load after another of ambulances pulled up. The worst hit were being treated on the spot. Those that could be moved were being brought to the Royal first, and the overspill would end up in the City Hospital.

Eithne saw a man who had been brought in, sitting calmly.

'Joe Molloy?' she asked him, but he did not hear her as his eyes stared past, reliving the blast. She tried another who nursed a bandaged head.

'Joe Molloy?'

'That's not me, love.'

'Did you see him? Do you know him?'

He looked at her and became agitated, trying to remember something. 'I'm . . . . ' he shook his head and trailed off absently.

It was hopeless. There was so much confusion. Nurses ran, taking names and checking identification.

'Most of these will sit for an hour over a cup of tea and go off home. Superficial shock,' a UDR man said.

'This is the last lot coming now.' He nodded towards the door as an ambulance pulled up. 'They sent out four to pick up casualties. If your husband's not in this lot he's probably still down there.'

'Has anyone else been killed?' she asked. 'Was anyone killed in the bombing?'

'That I couldn't tell you, but there are some numbers to ring.'

'Yes, I know,' she cut him short and ran out to the ambulance, waiting to see the grim-faced people who came out of it: women wrapped in blankets, men weeping openly; no children. Eithne saw no children. She heard voices wailing.

'Oh God. Oh God, I saw a body being torn apart. I'll never forget, never.'

'Jesus, Mary and Joseph, it was awful, awful . . .'

Someone else was screaming 'No, No, No,' over and over, wanting to prevent the memory by shouting.

'We'll put this lot under sedation and keep them in overnight,' Eithne overhead a doctor saying to a group of nurses. She tried to tell herself that Joe was dead, so that she could rehearse how it would sound before someone really told her.

'He's dead,' she told herself, imagining what she ought to say.

Over the road, outside the church, a black taxi pulled up. Eithne ran towards it. People were squeezing up inside to let others in.

'I can take you as far as Castle Street,' the driver told her. 'The traffic's all been diverted in town.'

'Have you been anywhere near it? Near the explosion? What's it like?' an old woman with three Co-op bags asked.

'No, love,' he said, beginning to pull away from the kerb, 'but town has come to a standstill.'

'My husband was there,' Eithne said slowly. 'He was working on the site next to the shop where the bomb went off.'

There was a hush as the travellers in the taxi looked at her and looked away.

'Good God Almighty!' the old woman said. 'I'll pray for you.'

'Aye,' said another, 'we all will, love,' and she squeezed Eithne's hand.

The driver leaned back and shouted over his shoulder.

'I'll take you around the back if I can, try and get you as close to it as they'll let me, OK?'

'Thanks,' she muttered, feeling tears begin to fill her eyes.

'They ought to gas the lot of them, if you ask me. One lot's as bad as the other.'

'It's always innocent people who suffer,' the old woman said. 'There are no winners at times like these.'

Evelyn was breathless. She had run almost the entire distance from College Square on. Now she stood across the street from Ainsworth's. It was a burnt-out shell, smouldering as firemen trained hoses on it. Olive-green army screens had been erected at various points where the rescue workers were already bringing out bodies. She stood numbly. She heard bits of disjointed stories which lodged in her mind like shrapnel.

'It was packed, they say, when the bomb went off. The warning was delayed.'

'The blast caught them on the hop.'

'Afternoons are the busiest times there you see. . . . '

'I looked up and saw a sort of yellow fireball. All flames. I was just after coming out of the chemists, a few seconds earlier and I might have been across the road and in the middle of it.'

'You're that lucky to be standing here.'

A UDR man was shouting through a megaphone for people to stand well back and let the rescue workers through.

Evelyn walked along the pavement over bricks and rubble, she peered into the crowd, hoping to see Porter's face. It had started to rain. Suddenly she knew that she could not stand there watching. She wanted to turn and run away from the scene. She did not have the strength to witness what was happening. She remembered that he had arranged to meet her back at the hospital. She would turn back. First she would check the car park, if the car was still there, then she would return to the Royal and sit it out. 3.30 he had said. She would wait until then, then she would dial one of those numbers. Coldly she turned her back.

Eithne ran from the taxi. It was raining steadily. Strange because she had not noticed it begin, and it had been dry when she left the hospital. Opposite the bomb site the gutters already ran with streaks of blood in the muddy rainwater. She looked away, but she could hear it gurgling down the grid. She had not wanted him to take the week's work in the city. From the start, she felt that there was something unsafe about it. So what if he was just a brickie? He was working on a yard that belonged to a company which regularly did work on RUC stations. It did not take a genius to work out that such a concern would be targeted. But why shoot someone for being in the wrong place at the wrong time.

Then she saw him on the corner. She was as near hysterical as she ever remembered being. He was standing very still. All around him everything blurred, turning slate-grey, and he was weeping, standing on his own. He did not see her until she was upon him and all he said was, 'They shot Davey', then he looked away.

One of his work mates came up.

'I saw him fall,' he told Eithne, taking up the story her husband was unable to continue.

'I saw him fall. He was out at the front and the car drew up. I heard a single shot a few seconds later, and the men in the car yelled at us to clear the yard; that the whole lot was going to go up. Davey was lying there. We ran. No one tried to move him, he was lying out there on the street. Blown to Christ knows where. He was in the wrong place. He saw them. That's all. In the wrong place.'

Eithne felt relief. Her mind was free of hate because it was not her husband who was dead. Now she could see the underlying meaning to the act. She was almost peaceful as she helped her husband away from the scene.

In the Royal Victoria Hospital, the other woman sat waiting for the hands of the clock to move. Beads of sweat stood out on her brow. She was a polite woman, but as the fingers moved to 3.30 she retched and spat on the ground, not caring who saw. Her spittle tasted sour and she thought that she might vomit. The hands moved slowly while she reminded herself that she had never wanted anything to do with their politics and neither had he. Fear bit into her. As she grew desperate the oddest thought screamed in a voice she did not want to recognize. The unpremeditated thought ran riot; she felt disgust for it, but when she tried to put words on it, the words which came easiest and gave her the most relief said 'Catholic scum'. She thought she would vomit.

'Catholic scum,' she mouthed, and spat again.

Agnes Dei

It was the Sunday morning procession to ten o'clock service. Along the main street was the noise of voices chattering, and the jealously shouted hellos to those returning from early mass who had gained the remainder of their day free of obligation. Women rearranged their hats awkwardly and children in stiff shirts and clothes 'not for playing in' walked miserably behind their parents, out in this once-weekly, formal airing. The majority found it boring. Many found it difficult to appear together as a family for as long as the service lasted, including in this the walk to and from church. They struggled to maintain the illusion of peaceful coexistence, all wanting to be seen as good Catholic families.

'The family that prays together stays together,' the parish priest was fond of saying; so fond that he had it written up over the notice board at the back of the church.

Later, over the Ulster fry with the greasy Sunday sausages, the arguments would begin anew as families found one day of each other's company unendurable. Sundays were awful because there were no distractions except routine indigestion from the late and heavy breakfasts. For many the day was spent cramped into their small houses, irritably studying the habits of their brothers, sisters, wives or husbands. Supposed to be a day of rest, a day for quiet reflection, it was instead the day on which

77

slumbering arguments awoke, the day on which life-long hatreds were cemented.

One family making its way to Saint Aloysius' that morning were no more remarkable than the rest, but for the fact that they only said 'Good Morning' in reply and walked a fraction stiffer than most. They stared ahead, continuing their humourless way to church. If people thought them different, no one passed comment; maybe they thought the wife an odd fish, but no one knew them well enough to make any further judgement. The wife in question hated all others with a depth of feeling which was surprising from her bland appearance; despite the fact that she did not know them, she had a profound dislike for the members of her parish.

She was sure she heard them talking about her as she walked past. She thought that she always looked stupid because she was short and fat and had difficulty appearing elegant and this, she had learnt, was reason enough not to be respected. She understood that her shortness encouraged people to look down on her; lack of height brought with it a lack of esteem. She tried wearing high heels, but they made her legs look ridiculous and her knees grotesque. High heels did not flatter her. Her legs were too spindly. Not that she would have wanted legs like a footballer's, muscle-bound and thick. That's what games do for you, she thought.

All her life she hated organized sport. At school she had been useless, ducking whenever a ball came her way, and she was mortified at the swimming baths and never learned to swim. They used to laugh at her in class because she was so hopeless. She was terrified of running, choosing to let buses pass her rather than risk getting out of breath in public. She had a fear of being red and flushed, it embarrassed her. She dreaded sweating. She became stiff and awkward, and grew to hate anyone who looked comfortable or at ease with their body.

'They think that they own the place,' she always said.

She hated how anyone could walk into church with their arms swinging naturally by their sides and genuflect without cracking their knees.

'They make me sick,' she said. 'Fancy ones, all dressed up for church, it's not supposed to be a fashion show.'

No matter what she wore, she felt the same. She wore dark colours, hoping to recede. She hated those who did not.

'Did you see the look of that one!' she would exclaim after mass. 'All dolled out in pink! Pink! I ask you. . . . Fancy showing herself off like that. And without a jacket, out in her figure. It's not right coming to church all dressed up, there ought to be a rule about it, that would soon put those flighty ones in their place.'

She knew they only came to church to see and be seen. When could they have had time to pray between trips to the dry cleaners and the hairdressers, and who knows what else? She believed that those who were not fat were vain because they dieted. It made her sick.

'Those fancy ones must starve themselves – what's the point in being thin and miserable, making yourself ill by not eating? I'd rather be fat and happy,' she said jealously.

Lots of things disgusted her. She did not like many people. Eventually her feelings spread to her family. The distrust she had for strangers absorbed her feelings for her children as she watched them grow and turn into people she no longer knew. She had no real control over them; they had separate identities and would not take her orders seriously.

'Honour thy father and thy mother!' she would scream, and the more she insisted the further they pulled away from her. She tried to turn them against the neighbours. She warned them not to get too friendly outside the family.

Sundays were this mother's weekly trial. When the ordeal was over and she was back home she would attack everything she had seen with a vehemence that tore to shreds the myth of Sundays, day of rest. For her family, the after mass discussion was as much a ritual as the mass, and part of their weekly obligation, to hear the tirade of abuse from her lips. They too hated Sundays. Agnes, the eldest girl, would absent herself as much as possible from her mother's company. She would spend the day pretending to read or study so that she could remain locked in silence. Fionualla, the next in age, usually spent Sundays humouring her mother. She had ambitions for canonization. The twins played football in the yard, or fought with each other and told tales. Loyalty did not rate highly with them. Their father bit his nails and cracked his knuckles.

This particular Sunday was the worst yet. Agnes walked slowly behind the rest of her family, who did not notice that she trailed. She watched her mother's awkward, graceless walk, feet spread out like a duck. She was wearing those white shoes which Agnes knew where a mistake. Her mother always had trouble with her feet and would have been more comfortable in the flat lace-ups she normally wore, but for some reason she put herself through this regular discomfort each Sunday. That and the gloves. Agnes winced. Nobody else's mother wore white gloves. She only ever wore one, the other always scrunched up in the gloved hand, leaving the bare one free to carry the patent handbag. Agnes felt that it too was a mistake.

Sometimes, when her mother was being especially spiteful, Agnes had the temptation to yell back at her that if she were to stand in front of a mirror herself and see her own shoes and her precious gloves, she might stop complaining about women wearing pink and looking dressed up. But she never did. It was one of the reasons her mother raced home after the end of mass, why she hated the groups of people standing around on the pavement after it had finished. She called it the gathering of the clans and said it made her sick. Agnes thought it must be nice to stand around talking to friends on Sunday mornings.

'Standing around showing off!' her mother said. Having

friends was synonymous. It was just as well then that her parents had none, they would never err along the lines of pride.

The girl was panicking. Her stomach heaved. She had forgotten her trouble for a few seconds.

Anxiety was like that; letting other things come into your mind and blocking everything out for a second, before the chief worry presented itself again in a further develop-ment, with another, more disastrous consequence attached to it.

What would her mother say when it was discovered? The shame would shrivel her up. Everyone would talk about it. Agnes was desperate. Once her mother knew the awful secret she harboured, her Sunday morning agony would be spread over the entire week, and it would continue for eternity until her mother died, condemned and ashamed.

Her mother would be unable to show her face again and she would say in years to come, 'I've got my daughter to thank for this disgrace'.

Her father would be quicker to act. He would kill her. It might be the only solution.

As the family reached the church, Agnes hesitated as if she had not reached a decision about something and would have liked more time to consider before committing herself to the church's interior. None of her family noticed. The heavy wooden door was wedged open, held in place by the careful positioning of a single brick which one of the Knights of Saint Columba had seen to earlier. It was part of the church's attempt at lay involvement. The priest drew up lists and made rotas which the Knights took over by putting their names forward in a block. At every mass a representative would be on hand to pass the collection boxes round with a granite-mouthed look, not human in their performance of higher duties, which they alone had the importance to undertake; puffed up with religious esteem and showing their devotion by the punctual placing of a brick.

The family went through the arch of grey stone, rippling as they dipped their heads in turn in front of the statue of Saint Aloysius. The church was full of cold shadows as they walked noiselessly to their usual position, neither too far front nor too far back. It was not their style to go squarely up to the centre front, slap-bang, with knees almost touching the altar. Not like some people the wife could have named. They were reticent. They did not speak up in church. They did not shout out prayers, neither did they volunteer for church jobs; but they did not in return ask the church for anything. They did not seek prestige through the friendships of priests. The informal camaraderie with the clerics after mass was not for them. Of course Father Leach always nodded; 'Good to see you,' he would mutter as they passed into the street, but neither did his face break out into an unsolicited grin as it might when telling others the same.

The congregation rose swiftly as the celebrant came on to the altar. 'I will go to the altar of God,' the priest intoned, and they answered mechanically, 'The God of my gladness and joy.'

Agnes's voice did not help to swell the mumbling as people rose shuffling to their feet. People knocked against leather kneelers, bruised themselves and cursed softly. Everything echoed in the high vaulted ceiling.

Gladness and joy? she thought. How could she feel gladness and joy?

At sixteen Agnes felt worldly wise, more wise than her parents dreamed. Spurred by their example she held no romantic view of marriage. Despite herself she felt a slight chuckle. She was a woman with a woman's knowledge at last. It should have all stopped right there but she had made a miscalculation. She had rushed to gain knowledge of the secret life men and women shared. She imagined herself when she was older, in her twenties, starting out on the secret life, not as a novice but as a woman of the world. It was a safeguard. She did not want to be made to look like an idiot by anyone. But look what she had landed herself in. She was a fool.

She could not believe how she had let it go out of control. How could she have been so stupid to trust him? The way he talked as if she was soft for even worrying.

'Trust me,' he'd said and she, like a fool, believed him.

'I know how to avoid that.'

Bloody man of the world! And her thinking he knew what he was talking about. She ought to have followed her instincts. If only she had not been so green, she could have demanded that he use something, but she did not know whether he was or not. She had no skill in such a situation and as she floundered he took control.

Now she was certain that it had gone wrong; that he did not know anything, that he was as inexperienced as she was, the way he hurt her.

She tried to recall what happened but, like the event, her memory of it was fumbled. His breath had stunk of beer, it made her feel sickly, she had to turn her head away. He was heavy too, she had not accounted for that and it shocked her the way he lay on top, crushing and suffocating her. His knees bruised her thighs. Not that he cared. He was not gentle, he did not even speak to her after. The way he pretended that he had not known it was her first time, feigned ignorance of how painful it had been for her.

'If you'd said something I'd have taken it slower like,' was all he said, at last, after she had lain sobbing on the damp grass. Her silence irritated him.

'Well, how was I to know?' he demanded angrily when she did not reply. She wondered what difference it would have made. None now anyway.

Agnes stood up slowly with the rest of the congregation. Already she was feeling sick. That was a sure sign. She knew about women being sick with it. When her mother was carrying Gerald and Dominic it made her ill. Agnes caught her at it a few times. There would be nothing on the table and her mother, as white as the flour she kneaded for soda, with the dough still all over her fingers, would be out in the back retching over the sink. She said that the babies caused her sickness. But surely that did not happen this soon? It had only been two weeks.

It was after the local dance. Some of those men were like animals when they had the drink inside them. Pigs, drunken no-good pigs! They weren't all from the parish either. He wasn't. He told her that he usually attended Saint Finbar's. That meant that she would not see him at mass here and would not see him anywhere else.

'I confess to Almighty God.
To Blessed Mary ever a virgin,
To Blessed Michael the Archangel,
That I have sinned exceedingly,
In thought, word, and deed.'

She listened, feeling guilty. She wondered if she had the right to be present at mass because she still had not been to confession. She could not go to her own church. Father Leach would know her voice. It would mortify her; he would think her a common slut and give her sly looks at mass. She was no better than the rough women who hung around the docks and went home with anyone for the price of a bottle of gin. The names her father had for such women made her face burn.

Hadn't she done the same thing going off with a man like that at the end of a dance?

'Dear God. Forgive me,' she prayed, knowing that it did not count until she made a full confession. The only way she could contemplate it would be to go to another church where nobody knew her. She would have to lie about where she was going. It was a sure way of knowing someone had something big on their minds when they went to another parish.

All the subterfuge would not save her; everyone would see her problem soon enough.

She was only four days late. It didn't necessarily mean that she was . . . but she felt sick with worry. She was always so regular, never like this. Was there anything she could do to help it along? Throw herself down the stairs or carry heavy weights? Didn't they always warn pregnant women about lifting loads? Maybe that would do the trick?

She had driven herself mad the last few days every time she went to the lavatory, inspecting her drawers for blood spots. Women had ways of dealing with such things. There was some kind of pill you took after, but where did you get them? There was nobody she could ask. Suppose it was all a mistake? She would have told somebody and everyone would know she had spoiled her priceless chastity, and for what? No man would want her if they found out, although that no longer seemed such an awful prospect.

Brutes. Rough coarse-smelling things they had between their legs. Heavy clammy bodies, foul beery breath. She looked sideways at her father. How could her mother endure that, night after night? Perhaps that's why they had warned her, because it was such a punishment after marriage.

She could travel to another town where no one would know her. But the thought of going up to a stranger in a chemist's and asking for such a thing made her cheeks burn. If only someone had told her where to get the things before the event. Not like this, in desperation. He said not to worry before he shoved himself into her and it hurt.

After, she tried to look at it out of the corners of her eyes while he rearranged his clothing. Curled like a one-eyed maggot, pink and hideous. Naked. There was nothing on it, nothing resembling those things she had heard about. One of the girls where she had a Saturday job said that men blew them up like balloons. Yes, that's what Theresa said, like balloons. Well, where was it? There was nothing left on the grass as testimony to their deed. Theresa said she had seen one in the park, before the keeper came round clearing up leaves and crisp packets.

Theresa had only left school that summer, yet she had an air of being much older than Agnes. She worked in the store all week and knew a lot about things Agnes had no idea of. She had two brothers, both older than her, they must have told her.

Agnes wondered if she could ask her when she was next in work, but she would have to do it without letting her suspect that she was worried.

'Hey Theresa, you know what you told me about men?'

She would start a conversation naturally without giving the game away and steer it round to doctors, then ask her whether she knew any who might help a girl who needed it. It would be difficult. In the first place she would be embarrassed just talking about such things, and Theresa was sharp, she'd be bound to suspect. She'd ask her why she was talking dirty. No, it wouldn't work. Better to be honest and swear her to secrecy. But could she trust her? For all she knew, Theresa might tell her own parents, or it might get back to the rest of the workers and then the employer would fire her for immoral acts while in his employment.

It was hopeless. She could write into one of those magazines and sign herself 'Desperate of . . .' and hope no one recognized that it was her. She could just put 'Desperate', and leave the place out. No one would suspect. She could not give them her address. She would have to burn the reply.

'Who was that letter from?' her father would ask and she would have to act soft.

'Which letter?'

'The one I saw you reading this morning.'

'Oh. That? Nothing, I burnt it,' and she would laugh lamely, pretending it was a joke. He would interrogate her until he discovered the truth, she would have no peace.

Maybe there was a number she could dial. She would

have to go to the call box with a purse full of coppers and keep an eye out that her father did not follow her. She could go through the directory and call up a doctor, any doctor. But with her luck she would probably end up with the best friend of their family practitioner, they all knew each other. If Doctor Foggarty found out what she had been asking then he would be round to her father like a shot. God, he was worse than the priest. That time she'd that itching down below; he had given her a lecture about loose morals and her sitting there like an eejit not knowing what he was talking about and as embarrassed as anything on account of where the itching was. Jesus, if it had been her armpit that was troubling her would he have gone on for so long, telling her to keep praying as she used the penicillin?

Suddenly Agnes was shaken back to the present. Everyone around her was standing up. She struggled to her feet hoping that she was in time with the congregation.

'I believe in one God,

The Almighty Father, maker of heaven and earth,

Maker of all things visible and invisible.

I believe in one Lord Jesus Christ,

The only begotten Son of God . . .'

She could not follow the prayer. The only part she heard clearly were the words 'was incarnate of the Virgin Mary by the power of the Holy Spirit'. Everything in the mass was about getting pregnant, she had never noticed before.

When they read out 'I look forward to the resurrection of the dead and the life of the world to come' Agnes missaid it, and looked forward to the new life to come and was terrified in case anyone overheard her.

She quickly bowed her head when the offertory bell sounded so that she might not catch a glimpse of the Host when the priest held it up; she was unclean, not worthy to observe the miracle accidentally.

'For this is the chalice of my blood – which shall be shed for you and many unto the remission of sins.'

If Christ shed his blood for sinners, why wouldn't he show compassion by causing hers to flow? She was praying for a miracle.

'Dear God,' she prayed, '. . . I will never do it again. I'll never commit this sin out of marriage. I swear that for ever after I will save myself. I will fast for the rest of the nine months to make it up to you, I promise, only please, please, spare me this. Dear Lord. My parents will kill me, well, my father will. He'll call me all sorts. I don't like to say the words to you, but my father will have occasion to sin because of me, he'll swear something terrible. I'll never be able to walk up the High Street again. Sweet Jesus, don't forget what happened to the Malachy girl. After they threw her out, she was never seen again and my father agreed with them for turning her out like that . . . he said that they were right because she was a rotten apple, the likes of which you wouldn't keep under a Christian roof, not if you didn't want the priest to stop calling. My dad said anyone going over that step would be tainted by her sin.

'I'll make sure Fionualla doesn't make the same mistake. I'll keep such an eye on her. I wouldn't corrupt her, I'd keep her straight. Amen.'

Agnes knew that there were homes for unmarried mothers and the finality of that made her feel faint. She caught the edge of the pew and heaved herself up on to the seat. It was hard to give even the appearance of following the mass. She stared vacantly around and tried to support herself in position by pushing the base of her spine against the hard wooden bench until she was secretly sitting. She hoped no one noticed. All around the walls of the church were the stations of the cross. Large oil paintings which had been donated so long ago without signatures that everyone had forgotten the name of the artist. A self-effacing penance for an indulgence. The one closest to Agnes read 'Jesus is scourged at the pillar'.

In some countries, she reasoned, they would do the same to her. A woman like herself might be whipped or stoned.

And for what? What pleasure had she had? It would be no hardship to save herself until she was married now that she knew what it felt like. If she had known, he would never have been able to talk her into it. These priests and nuns, making out like it was a whole big deal doing without it. God, they weren't missing anything. She would warn her sister.

Her eyes wandered around the walls. At the ninth station of the cross she read the inscription.

'Jesus meets the mourning women of Jerusalem'. 'Daughters of Jerusalem,' He said to them, 'weep not for me, but for yourselves and your children.'

She knew what He meant. Women might as well weep.

'Lord, I am not worthy to receive thee under my roof,' the altar boy intoned and Agnes realized with a jolt that she must not go to communion.

She clung back as the time approached to leave their pew and go to the altar. They always went to communion together every Sunday. She cursed herself for not being the first into the row because then she would have been the last out. Most likely her family would not have noticed until they returned, although there would be the same inquisition later.

'Why didn't you go to communion? What sin have you committed that your conscience is bothering you?'

She could not do anything out of the ordinary. Whenever she received a letter, her father had to know who it was from, where it had been posted, and he expected to be given a brief résumé of its contents. When she tried to tell him that some things were private, he got into a state, yelling about filthy secrets that she was ashamed of. You could never accuse him of being a man of little imagination.

The communion bell sounded. It was awful, they had to clamber over Agnes to get out, her sister, the twins, all looking at her in surprise and falling against her. Their father gave her an angry look and tripped over her foot. He swore under his breath and she thought that he was going to hit her, but he stopped himself just in time. One had to be in a state of grace to receive communion. The mother stood at Agnes's side, waiting for her to move. She did not realize that her daughter was standing back to let them through.

'Well, get a move on then!' She jabbed her with her elbow.

'I'm not going.'

'What?' asked the woman absently, and slowly as she realized what the girl had said, she turned to look more closely at her to discover which dreadful wrong was being harboured.

'What did you say?'

Agnes set her face and stared ahead. Her mother would not want a fuss, not in public, even if she could not understand why their usual routine was disrupted, she would continue as though nothing had happened until the end of mass. Agnes looked sullen, she bowed her head and arched her back in an exaggerated movement to allow her mother past. The woman had no choice but to keep moving before anyone noticed the delay in their row.

The priest walked down the altar steps and stooped to place the sacred host into the mouth of the first recipient, while the altar boy with bent back followed, holding the silver plate that had been polished and shined by one of the Handmaidens of Mary that morning. The phrase 'The Body of Christ' and the answer 'Amen' went along the line, repetitive and soothing.

Agnes sat back on the bench, isolated from the faithful. She was sweating and thankful for this lull in the mass. If she remained sitting throughout the rest of it she could pretend that she was sick, rather than face them at the end of mass without any alibi.

Fionualla grabbed her arm as she came back. 'Hey, are you OK?' she whispered.

Agnes nodded. 'I just feel a little nauseous that's all.'

She did not attempt to stand as the priest left the altar.

Slowly he walked down the steps flanked by his two servers in their black cassocks and white ruffs. It was the nineteenth Sunday after Pentecost. Father Leach wore the green altar vestments which had been painstakingly stitched by nuns of the Sacred Heart Convent. They were carefully hung up at the end of every mass, and taken for pressing each Sunday eve by one of the Handmaidens of Mary. The front panel of the vestments showed the four evangelists in embroidered circles, each one carefully couched down with gold thread; a labour of many long nights. The scribe, the eagle, the lion and the ox. The back panel showed the good shepherd. At the bottom of the garment there was a small embroidered lamb. All were worked neatly in cross-stitch.

It was considered an honour to take the robes home. This was how the women of the parish showed their responsibility, because they could be trusted to clean the priest's vestments. These handmaidens would vie with each other to see who accomplished the best result. Father Leach would thank them individually, with a few words of praise that made them each believe it was their particular touch he valued, their special knack with the iron. . . .

'Ah,' he would say with satisfaction as he took the tissue-wrapped parcel from one of them, 'I always know when you've pressed the robes, Annie, the cuffs are always so neatly turned'; or remark that someone was a perfectionist: 'I've never seen such impeccable ironing in all my days.'

Spurred on by his praise, the competition between them was rife.

The rota for altar duties was jealously guarded and if one handmaiden was late for any of her tasks, other eager handmaidens would gladly jump in, desperate to get up on the altar after the Host was removed to follow reverentially with their vacuum cleaners the carpet tracks where the priest had walked, or be allowed to do a nice arrangement of flowers for the middle altar.

Agnes's mother did not join the handmaidens, nor the

Ladies of Charity, and her father had not volunteered for the Saint Vincent de Paul. They were not a family who liked to get too closely involved with anything. They kept themselves to themselves.

'Ask no questions and you'll be told no lies,' their mother always said. It would have petrified her to be a member. She could not have gone up on to the altar before mass, to check the flowers in full view of the congregation, before the Host was in place. As soon as the little red side lamp was lit, the handmaidens scurried away from the altar, scared to touch the carpet with their unworthy feet. Agnes thought it was stupid to be so eager to clean and scrape and she was proud that her mother would not do so. Agnes would never have volunteered; not that she ever could now. Once she had pitied the handmaidens, now they could all pity her. If any of the Ladies of Charity tried giving her baby clothes she'd throw them in their faces. No, she would rather leave the parish than put up with that.

Her family knelt as the priest disappeared through the doors into the vestry, the starched white ruffs of the two altar boys following him. Her family always waited a reasonable time before leaving the church so that no one could say they rushed out, but they did not wish to overstay, and they certainly did not hang around. They walked silently out of church as if they were embarrassed for something that they had done. It was only when they had gone some distance down the street that they realized they were one short.

'Fionualla, run back and get that half-wit of a sister of yours.'

'What is wrong with the girl? She's more dead than alive this morning.'

Fionualla dutifully went back. She was concerned that Agnes might have fainted and was being stretched out on a bench by one of the altar boys. She dashed through the porch and saw her sister down by the Lady Chapel. She had stayed behind to pray for a special intention. As she walked down the aisle towards the statue of Our Lady she saw her sister stand up and cross towards the rack. Agnes dropped some coins into the box and lifted a candle from the pile, lit it and pressed it down to stand among the others. She knelt on the red-cushioned bench and bowed her head.

Fionualla felt the sudden heat as she approached the stand. She slipped behind the flickering candle flames, each one lit by a supplicant and left burning long after the prayer finished. Agnes had placed hers in the cleanest socket she could find, pushing it down firmly so that it might not fall or bend out of shape and burn down one side as some of the others. She wanted her intention to be as straight as possible, its smoke heavenwards.

The rivers of wax caught on the metal bars to cool and solidify into spontaneous sculptures. Fionualla thought those shapes were wonderful. When she was younger she used to play by dipping her fingers into the hot wax to take away the impressions in the soft petals which stuck to them. She remembered how Agnes tried to hold her hand over a flame once to punish herself for some transgression. She burnt the side of her arm before drawing it away. Fionualla tried to see if she was as brave but had pulled back flinching. That was when she knew she could never be a martyr.

The Lady Chapel had always been both sisters' favourite place to pray. It was a niche in the church where they would go after school and talk. Fionualla looked at the statue. It seemed to know and be tolerant of all their foibles, a half smile ever present on its cold lips. Agnes had dropped her head, unable to meet the blue gaze of its glass-chip eyes.

Her mouth moved in prayer. 'Heavenly Mother forgive me, for on earth there is no compassion.'

Fionualla was startled to see her sister in such an attitude, her body screaming for consolation. She presented

93

a figure both subservient and pleading. It was so unlike her. Agnes was never in awe of anything. Agnes was brave. Agnes was rash, the way she would rush in and do things. Agnes always went first, she had to have a go and Fionualla would watch and then decide if it was worth it.

Agnes plucked her eyebrows once, secretly at night, into two finely drawn crescents, one a lot smaller than the other. Fionualla could not even hold the tweezers when it was her turn.

'Does it hurt? Does it hurt?' she asked wincing.

'Sit still,' her sister ordered and she clutched the pillow with her fists and gritted her teeth. Agnes pulled out a single hair from Fionualla's brow and she screamed as the tweezers ripped away from her.

'Shut up, eejit! You'll wake Mum and Dad!'

But they could not stifle their laughter. Fionualla looked in the shaving mirror that Agnes held towards her. There was a red spot that felt itchy where the hair had been torn from the follicle. Agnes wanted to do the rest, but she wouldn't let her near her. One hair was the limit.

'Go away, it's agony!'

And it was Agnes who got into trouble with the nuns the next day.

It was Agnes who took them both to get their ears pierced at a jeweller's in town. Fionualla met her at the store where her sister worked on Saturdays and that girl from the shop came with them, Theresa. She had been terrified, but would not admit it in front of the older girl.

'I'm only having it done if they freeze my ears,' she whispered to her sister. 'I can't have it done without.'

Theresa told them that the jeweller's was closing down so they would be silly to pass up the chance as they were doing it cheap. Agnes said that once they had it done there was nothing their parents could do about it. If they forbade them to wear ear-rings, they could still wear studs secretly in bed to stop the holes closing over.

When they got to the shop, Fionualla saw that the man

was going to use a staple, one which shot straight into the lobe of the ear and didn't need freezing. She shuddered looking at it lying on the desk.

'It goes in so fast you don't feel anything. Honest,' Theresa said. 'It's how I had mine done.'

Even Agnes looked shocked.

'I'll go first,' and she sat in front of the mirror keeping an eye on Fionualla who had grown rather pale.

She watched Agnes wince twice. The man stood back, and there in her ears were two tiny golden studs. Agnes put her hand up and touched them experimentally.

'Well? Did it hurt?' Theresa asked triumphantly.

'It does smart a bit.'

'You mustn't take them out,' the man said, 'not until at least six weeks and you'll need to bathe them with salt water. They'll run at first, but after a few weeks you shouldn't see any more blood.' He dabbed the ears with cotton wool.

'Oh look,' Theresa said, leaning over to get a better view. 'Agnes, you're bleeding.'

Fionualla felt the shop grow dark and everything closed in around her. She came round with her sister slapping her face.

'You made a right fool of yourself,' she told her that night, glaring at her unpierced ears. And it was Agnes who was shouted at.

She precipitated most of the rows at home because she was the eldest. She wanted to fly, and her mother always said that she would clip her wings. It was Agnes who stood in doorways, kissing after the parish dances. It was Agnes who established the time that they should both come home. It was Agnes who took a drink from the bottle of whiskey they kept for the priest at Christmas and then topped it up with water.

One Christmas she smoked half a cigar, in the bathroom with the window open, and then she'd vomited into the lavatory bowl. Their mother was worried, thinking it was the turkey that was undercooked and they'd all go down with food poisoning. Fionualla couldn't keep her face straight, but Agnes was too ill to see the funny side. Her face was green, not quite like the holly they placed in corners of the room which managed to have a festive look. Agnes sat on the edge of the bath looking wretched. She had almost the same look on her face now, only this time she was kneeling with her hands clasped tightly in devotion. Fionualla had not seen her like this before.

She had to call her name twice before she looked round.

'Come on, dozy, we're all waiting.'

Agnes looked up at her sister, her lips kept moving hopelessly in prayer. '*Agnus Dei, qui tolis pecata mundi, miserere nobis.*'

She allowed her sister to lead her down the aisle. Before they stepped out into the light she sighed heavily and muttered again the prayer. 'Lamb of God, who takest away the sins of the world, have mercy on us.'

Fionualla took her sister firmly by the elbow and steered her out on to the pavement. Agnes went dumbly, knowing that she had relinquished her position for ever, and the younger girl, sensing her new authority, wondered what had happened to upset the rigid order at home. Whatever it was it made no sense, she thought, as she led Agnes out on to the bright street. In the sunlight the older girl blinked. She was blinded for a minute and Fionualla took her hand to steer her.

'I feel like I'm leading a lamb . . .' but something about Agnes's face stopped her from finishing the sentence.

Their mother was already out of sight, and it struck Fionualla that her sister looked like she wanted to hide, or at least get home quickly in time for the slaughter.

The Strange Case of the Vanishing Woman

The doctor pulled off his transparent plastic glove with the deftness of one practised in such movements. He threw it into the pedal bin and began to wash his hands. He soaped them slowly, bringing them to a full lather under the warm tap, and rinsed carefully before repeating this procedure once more. He dried his hands methodically on a paper towel and crumpled it between his clean palms. With his left foot, he pressed again on the pedal and tossed the blue ball of paper after the glove, noticing for the first time that the bin was full. The missile landed squarely on the rubbish, then rolled forward. He watched it apprehensively. It settled, and he quickly released the pedal so that the bin would close. He would have preferred it to snap smartly shut, but being over-full it could do no more but rest at an angle on the layers of cotton wool, disposable gloves and paper towels, holding them in place in its loose bite.

'Cervical erosion,' he said. 'Nothing to worry about. It's very common, very common.'

He looked bored. She wished it was something exciting. He must listen to the same cases every day.

'You can get down now,' he said, and went behind the curtain.

She edged uneasily off the examination table. She was scared of heights. Her feet touched the polished lino and began to skid away from her. She put them up on the set of metal steps and sat balancing, looking for her roll-ons. She was sure that she had put them with her tights. She could not see them. As she stepped down her foot turned under. She fell sideways, catching the sharp edge of the cupboard with her hip. The metal speculum rang against the sides of the galvanized bowl as the table top vibrated.

'Jesus, Mary and Joseph, I'll be black and blue.'

She steadied herself against the bed.

'Mother of God!' she whispered, and at the same moment saw her roll-ons peeping out from under the cupboard. A miracle.

'Sweet Jesus, give me strength,' she thought as she began to wriggle into them. She was sweating and they stuck to her. Flustered, she lost her grip. The roll-ons sprang away from her, snapping back into a solid roll of elastic encircling her thighs.

She was certain that she was taking the longest to dress of all the patients that he had seen that morning, but hurrying made it worse. The more she snatched at the roll-ons, the more resistant they became. There was nothing else for it; slowly she took control and eased them off completely. She shook them wildly and straightened them out trying to keep calm; her breath was coming in gasps. She bent down, and felt her face get hot as blood rushed to her cheeks. She poked her flabby white stomach which stuck out like a little cushion and holding open the roll-ons, she eased it into the elastic casing.

'It's not decent going around without a girdle,' she thought. 'You could catch a wild cold that way. Leave something off that you were accustomed to wearing and the next thing you know – rheumatoid arthritis.'

She pulled the zip of her skirt together and slipped on her shoes.

'Which contraceptive method do you . . . did you use?' the doctor asked.

She had only just stepped out from the privacy of the

curtain, but she almost turned back. Now what was making him ask that, she wondered? If it was the old doctor he wouldn't be asking such stupid questions, he would not have dreamt of it. What did this young one take her for indeed? And after all these years when she had relied on God alone and the rhythm method. Not that she had to bother now.

'Were you taking the pill for any length of time?' he asked, looking up, seeing for the first time her expression. He knew then that he had made a mistake. If they would only fill in their religious background along with the rest of the details on their medical records, it would at least stop him putting his foot in it, he thought angrily. It might give him a bit more to go on instead of all this fishing about, watching their reactions. He was forever saying the wrong thing since he had taken over Doctor Cleary's practice. He tried to recover the sentence.

'I only asked because it's a fairly common thing in women who have been on the pill for any length of time. It's a response to oestrogen. Entirely normal in pregnancy, we don't have to worry about that, do we?' He smiled, hopefully, because she might see that it was a joke, but she was solemn.

'I shouldn't think so . . .' She just stopped herself from calling him Father, as she did anyone in authority.

'When was your last period?' he asked.

She thought hard. Was it last summer when they had been on holiday, or since? She really ought to write her dates down, but she had always been haphazard, even in the days when it mattered. She would hardly change now.

She did not have time to say anything, for just as she was about to open her mouth, at the exact moment as though he had timed it, his brisk, efficient tone cut across her unspoken word.

'Ah, they're not too frequent now, are they?' he read off the record card he held in front of him.

'Let's see . . . over a year now? Well, you might just see another one before it's all through.'

Before it's all through? She was puzzled; would she be all through in a year, locked in the cabinet marked confidential?

'When were you born?'

She opened her mouth again, but before she could say the date, before she even got her mouth and tongue properly positioned to begin the first sound, with her tongue pressed against her palate for the nasal nineteen hundred, he had answered for her.

'That seems about right,' he muttered. 'About right.'

He continued to examine her this way, reading the answers off the card, while she stared out of the window.

A copper beech overhung it, blocking out much of the daylight from outside. The scrap of garden it stood in was untidy, with litter blown in from the road. Nobody looked after it and weeds grew on what was once a lawn. Funny that she had not noticed the beech as she had walked in, for she had passed right next to it. She realized how worried she must have been, not to have seen how red it was. Shame about the garden. They ought to get a gardener. She never had a garden. She thought it must be wonderful, to go outside and still be in your own home, to know that you could sit quietly in the open air and not be pestered by strangers and other people's children; to go privately into the street. She only knew the feel of parks and pavements, municipal, dry and dusty. She only knew staring public places.

Every holiday that she went on had the same feel about it – loud and open in someone's awful bed and breakfast, where they wanted you out so that the house would return once again to their own, with no strangers dragging suitcases along the landing. Out into the glaring promenades and the rows of watchful deckchairs.

'You must think everyone is looking at you. Nobody is, nobody cares,' her husband said. She could not explain, it was a feeling, not an event. He accused her of turning odd, he looked at her queerly.

'Is it that thing. You know, when women are getting on?'

Blind he was. She was already well into the menopause and he had never noticed. She felt that she could disappear in a wreath of smoke and still he'd call out, 'What's for dinner?' If he blinked, she would be gone in that second when his eyelids closed. When he turned his back she disappeared. He never knew how she played with him, reappearing in the nick of time as he turned round to look at her.

The room was silent, she spun to face the doctor who was looking at her the way her husband sometimes did.

'Is that all right?' he repeated.

She nodded. The doctor waited. He must have asked her something which was not on the record.

'Oh yes,' she said, 'that's fine,' and she smiled in the hope that he might not have noticed. She took the prescription he held out to her.

'Just give it a couple of weeks and if it hasn't cleared by then, I'll do a swab.'

'The erosion?' she asked.

'No, the infection. It will clear, hopefully, with flagyl. The erosion is nothing to worry about. You can live with that.'

She folded the prescription carefully and put it inside her purse. As she walked through the door she heard the buzzer sound and the light bulb lit up over it, showing that this room was free. The next patient to be called was standing in the waiting-room, sorting out hats, coats, a handbag and a push chair as she walked through. It must become monotonous she thought, day in day out.

She wondered what women used to do in the days before antibiotics. In the old days women must have got the same infections surely? But then they probably did not have time to notice, especially there. God, her own mother would have been horrified if they had even suggested it;

go on, have a look, it won't bite, look and see for yourself. And God Almighty, weren't they telling the young ones now in school to use mirrors. That's what the woman next door told her, but then she was a Protestant and their way of education was totally different. The nuns at Saint Xavier's would hardly tell her daughter that.

She walked home, relieved but thoughtful. Somehow she had expected more; after all, she had worried about cancer, there was so much of it about. Her sister-in-law had to have a hysterectomy and then Mrs Sullivan's daughter, only just married she was when they discovered it. Terrible, she was such a lovely girl too. You never knew when God was going to try you; that's what she always said. Testing your faith by endurance. Now that she knew the verdict to be a straightforward infection that could be cleared with antibiotics, she felt strangely let down. It would be something to rush home and announce 'Cancer!' or 'I'm going to die!'. Her husband might hear that.

Not that she wanted to be ill, but this was really nothing to tell him and she would like him to see her and listen to her, instead of making her feel like the invisible woman.

That must be one of the advantages of having a garden. That private space where she could be alone; no one to ignore her and no strangers to look through her while their eyes erased her from the landscape.

She decided that she would go in the house proudly and tell her husband what she had, this thing that her doctor reckoned she could live with. At least if she confronted him with the facts, presented him with some pronouncement, he might not ignore her, but would have to listen for as long as she chose to speak, sounding each individual letter slowly. Cervical erosion. She tried saying it different ways, drawing out the gaps between each syllable. It represented the complete amount of time allotted to her, so she would make the best of it before his attention shifted back to the television. He carried on as if she was not there. That would be a fine thing she thought, if only she could disappear, but he would probably not notice that either. It was only when she had walked all the way home that she realized with regret that once again she had passed under the red copper beech without seeing it.

That evening she leafed through the family dictionary. It was a fairly hopeless one with pictures, bought when the girls were younger. She thought that it might not have the word and was surprised to find it standing out from the page. She would tell him as soon as she understood what it meant exactly, the true nature of the word in all its variations. She would draw it out, pull and stretch it, dazzle him with her lengthy knowledge.

'It's nothing to worry about,' she would say, 'it's just something I will have to live with without ever knowing that it's here.'

She heard her voice coolly giving him the news, repeating what the doctor said, 'without ever knowing'. If only she was not given to daydreaming she might have heard what else he said. He might have told her how to live with it, told her how she could expect to manage, given her some special hints on how to survive; and all the while she had been staring out at the tree, thinking about her last holiday.

She looked at the word on the page, squinting her eyes at the small print. Her sight blurred, but the heavier typeface of the heading commanded her to look.

Erosion
Erode
of acid, current, course of events.
eat away, destroy, gradually wear out.
2. become eroded.
3. Erodible, erosion, erosive (rodere, ros, gnaw).

She re-read it. To be eaten away. Well, she had wanted something exciting to tell him; she had dreamed cancer and been punished with total erosion. She had dared to tempt fate.

'Eat away, destroy, gradually wear out.'

At least the doctor had got something right, she was certainly worn out. But now she saw the magnitude of her condition she realized with horror that she would have to break the news gently to her husband. She felt that she barely understood it, as the weight and length of the word coiled about her and stretched outward; how could she speak of it?

'Rodere, ros, gnaw.'

The words bit into her already. She could feel the letters like sharp little teeth on the word, gnawing her insides. She closed the book heavily. She was stupefied and could not move but she knew that her stillness was only external. She knew that inside, fifteen sharp letters worked away like blades, not losing any time as they devoured her in an internal frenzy. She was disintegrating, being ground down to a fine powder which might blow away like dust, leaving hollow empty spaces. She was being erased permanently this time, not just in the reflections of people's eyes. Parts of her would become transparent and parts of her would disappear. It was just a matter of time until the gaps joined up, just a matter of time before there was nothing left, not even a relic. How long might it take? If she was vanishing, her body being removed from the inside out, it would only be a matter of time before her surface disappeared.

Day after day, she became aware of the changes taking place inside her. She alone knew how much less of her there was. The particles were minuscule, no one else would notice. She could not tell him what it was. She would lie awake at night listening to the silent house, and all the time she could hear the teeth moving, crunching and grating. She kept her hands over her belly so that he might not hear the sounds of her eradication. Or she would lie face down in the pillow, so her belly would be muffled by the mattress. He never once woke up. She wondered what the end would be like? Would her outside cave in when there was nothing left between the body walls? She would be a husk at last, a husk that might wither and decompose as all organic life.

It was a month after she first saw that word when she tested her stomach by prodding. Flatter, definitely flatter. She put a hand on one of her breasts. Almost nothing. Letting her hand run back towards her belly in desperation, she punched herself and felt her knuckles dig in. There was nothing on the other side, no flab, no muscle, but emptiness, the skin holding back the air which would pour through. Her belly was concave. Now, that was a difference. She weighed herself. She was lighter by a ridiculous amount. She wept for the past when she had wanted to diet and tame her round belly, and now she was succeeding in a way she did not want. Her entrails were disintegrating.

At the greengrocer's the assistant looked through her. 'Who's next?' he asked, and as she stepped forward, someone knocked her out of the way, or seemed to stand inside her because she could not step away and the other simply stood where she had been. When she opened her mouth to ask for a cauliflower, she heard someone else ahead of her. No one noticed, no one saw her leave, as no one had seen her enter the shop. Her voice was getting smaller and smaller. At confession the previous Saturday, when she started the customary 'Bless me father for I have sinned,' the priest continued saying his devotions behind the grille. Quietly intoning in a hypnotic voice, he was unaware that anyone sat in the confessional box. She had to knock to get his attention and he was puzzled by her voice. She shouted, and he could only just hear her. He asked her to speak up.

At mass on Sunday, she was drowned by the chorus and her voice died. On Monday, a bus pulled away from the stop leaving her sprawled on the pavement. No one saw her attempts to board. Her family paid her even less attention. She reckoned that she would disappear so completely that she would vanish, even from their memories.

It no longer seemed odd to her. That must be the nature of erosion, to take away any lingering ideas. On Wednesday, she could not find her knitting, she had left it in the sideboard cupboard months ago. It had become a bit of a joke because she had been knitting the same jumper for almost two years and the wool had changed shades. She thought that she might finish it and leave it as a lasting tribute to her existence. But when she went to look for it, it had gone. Her family were already clearing away her remains. On Thursday, she was terrified to open the wardrobe in case they had thrown all her clothes out. Not that she wore them, everything was too big. She went around in the same grey-coloured skirt and cardigan for weeks. When the waist became too big, she took it in with safety pins. She used to be a smart dresser, always choosing bright colours. Now she felt that the greyness suited her disintegration because it was not a colour, it was nothing but a tone which, like her, covered an empty space.

On Saturday morning, she stood on the scales in the bathroom. She was naked. He shouted in through the door. She paid no attention. She did not attempt to answer, but stepped lightly up on to the scales a second time to make sure. There must be something of her left if there was enough for him to find and yell at. Again she looked at the dial. It was impossible. She fiddled with it, jumped off and on as heavily as she could, but the needle did not move. It read the same each time. Nought. She weighed nothing. She stood down on to the rug. It's thick pile felt soft to her bare feet.

'How long are you going to be in that bloody bathroom!'

Her feet made no depression on the pile. The pink shaggy rug pushed up between her toes, but more than that, its pink fluff pushed right through her feet. The outlines of her ankles vanished as she stared. Air streamed through her calves. Air poured through her body. Overnight, in the dark, the gaps had been joining up like a jigsaw dismantling. In the morning, light streamed through what had once been her body. She was sure it had been there.

'Will you get a move on for Christ's sake!' he yelled impatiently through the door, but she could not answer him, she had no voice, no faculty for speech.

She felt herself lift and float. She wanted to cry with delight at the wonderful sense of freedom, but she had no tears. She experienced joy, warm all over, and she wanted to laugh because she understood how her soundless laughter was everywhere. Whatever she felt, she became. She was the laughter, she was the happiness, she was the freedom as she floated out through the tiny window.

On the other side of the door, her husband rattled the handle to the empty room.

Drop Stars Fall
In Unmarked Places

It had grown dark while the old woman sat at the window. The black heifer in the field vanished except for its four white hooves. Small things took shelter underground, and the hunter, with eyes lit, trotted on four dainty feet around the hen houses, sniffing for stragglers. The air smelt good, clear, with the frozen stars like icy points in blackness. As she watched, one raced away from its course to plummet earthwards, where it would lie until morning thawed the soil and melted its brittle star spikes. Shooting stars were common in that part of the northern hemisphere. They said it was because they were closer to heaven. When she was a child, the old woman searched for drop stars but she never found one. They told her that Molly McGurk was a star child because her hair was so blonde, odd for these parts. That was long ago when she had been a small dark child, earth-coloured like the rest, as if the night was always in them. Now her hair was silver-white, making her visible against the sky by her own bright star point.

The labourers were finished for the day, the shovels hung in the smaller barn.

They filtered away from the farm, leaving Stephan isolated in his maleness, awkward with his great muscular shape. He cast the biggest shadow on the farm at night. He irritated her. The great gombh of a thing! Even when he was a boy she had not liked him; she used to think that he was a simpleton, he was always that much slower than the other children. Now he ordered men about, but she could well imagine how they laughed behind his back; honest, decent workers being told what to do by an omadhaun! How he managed to give orders was beyond her, when he could not control his wife. Her granddaughter would sit down with that great gombh of a husband and work out what they would spend money on and what improvements would be made. In her day, no woman of the house sat down with men and told them what needed doing, and never discussed their rates of pay. It was Nora's idea to bring the good furniture out from the parlour, she did not believe in keeping the best only for Sundays and the priest's visits. Things were changing. They were born into different times as though by lottery. When she was a woman of twenty-eight she had to ask for permission to get married, going to Sean like a schoolgirl, and he stood up, with his hair combed, all formality, and asked her what kind of a man he might be, although he had known him all his life.

'Will he beat you or what?' he said, 'because I won't stand for that.'

That's how it was and she had counted herself lucky that her father was dead. If he had been alive he would have refused, he would never have given his consent, but would have kept her at home to cook and wash for him, oh yes. But her brother wanted the best for her. He kept an eye on her after their mother died, all careful when she got to marriageable age. Not that he should have worried. She dreaded the act of consummation; it was her worst fear, drummed into her horribly by her mother.

Stephan would not have lasted five minutes with her brother. He was a proper man, the kind you did not see nowadays, a dying breed that would all be forgotten, like herself. In her bones she felt that this might be her last winter. But she had thought that before when she had taken pneumonia in that damp place and they had brought her to stay here. To everyone's surprise she had recovered.

In the dark window she watched the reflection, as across the room Nora picked up her baby and suckled it. Lovely it was to be first-time mother. She could remember how those precious months felt when she would wait for the cry as her baby woke, raising its bald head from side to side, following any sounds. The milky yeasty smell, the tiny hands reaching out. Later it all became drudgery. There were too many babies, one after the other. Nora said the little one was special, but the old woman knew that a son was what a farm needed. There was plenty of time. The old woman watched now as her granddaughter rubbed the baby's back with a slow circular movement, over and over until at last they heard the croak, like a frog's, deep in the belly and the mother knew she could put her back down to sleep. Christ help her when the others start coming, she won't have the time to be moon-faced with pleasure; she would have the smile rubbed out of her face, a half-remembered stain hinting at the feeling long gone, and in its place old carbolicky memories. The old woman's lips stretched taut, and her fine skin cracked with her smudge of a smile, baring her teeth, which were long and brown; not stained with memories, but her one vice — snuff and the odd bit of tobacco, in private. She was never a drinker, a pioneer like her brothers who saw what drink did. Their father's life was made worthless through a haze of alcohol. A screen, he needed, from the past. A way of not looking back. He died an alcoholic, wretched and unforgiving.

Stephan was fond of a drop, but he knew when to draw the line. He might be a half-wit, but she had never seen him stupid on alcohol; God forbid, he'd be completely witless. Her lips split in a dry laugh.

She forced her back straight with difficulty and moved away from the window where she had sat for a long time in the same position. She grasped the table edge and

110

heaved herself across the kitchen, disguising her breathless-
ness by coughing. She knew they would have her invalided
as soon as look at her, and she needed dignity even if it
killed her. She wanted to go when she was ready, without
their attempts to prolong her life into senility, into a
deathlike existence, kept breathing by their care and attention. Now her granddaughter was probably wondering if
she had intended to sit for so long in one place or had
remained there because everything took her longer to do.
It was a bit of both.

She was searching the sky, and wanted to do it
thoroughly. She was counting the stars. She knew that
they would laugh at her, so she never told them why. But
there was a brighter star lately because the little one was
born. For each soul there is a star. Those that plummet
earthwards are lost. The night her sister died, two stars fell
together. Eileen's soul had another clinging to it. The old
woman felt chilled at the memory. She wanted comfort.
She wanted warmth after such a cold dark sky. She seated
herself by the fire and stared at the red and orange embers.

'Another shovelful of coal wouldn't hurt it now,' she
coaxed.

'No, I expect not,' Nora said, and threw a few lumps on
to the fire.

'Here. Let me fix a cushion up for your back.'

Nora's hands were as quick as her words. The old one
was pinned while the young hands deftly plumped up
cushions and smoothed out creases.

'There now.'

She held her grandmother and felt the empty reed ready
to snap with age. Her hands sensed the terrifying fragility.
Even the woollen garment she wore caught on Nora's
fingers like sharp dry splinters.

'Better?' Nora asked.

'Aye, better.'

The old one sank back tiredly. She closed her leathery
eyelids. All this fussing. They had her tortured. She wished

they would let her be. It was not like this in the old days. Then they just left them in a back room to die, let them go peacefully instead of stretching out their final years. Now her death was overdue. She felt it approach and turn her bones to chalk, but she kept quiet. It was her secret.

She heard her granddaughter calling her. Had she fallen asleep? That was one thing about getting old, she chuckled to herself, and began to sing.

'Poor aul Dicey Riley she has taken to the sup . . .' She beat the time with her fist on her knee.

'Poor aul Dicey Riley she will never give it up.

It's off each morning to the hock.

And she goes in for another little drop,

Ah the heart of the poor aul Dicey Riley.'

She knew she had missed something out, was it 'In the morning up she gets'? . . . Who used to sing that now, round at the old place?

'She walks along Fitzgibbon Street with an independent
    air.

And then it's down by Summerhill, and the people stop
    and stare . . .'

God rest her; it was Sean's wife. Round like a little barrel she was.

'She says "It's nearly half past one,

And it's time again for another little one,"

Ah the heart of the rule is Dicey Riley!'

. . . and she would sing that and laugh, and her plump body would shake under her flowery dress.

Yellow it was. The colour didn't suit her. It was a wedding and she got up and sang that, and them all pioneers, never taking so much as a drop in their lives. Didn't they laugh after. All dead now. A good woman that, but yellow made her look sick, someone should have told her. The recollection made her laugh, but not with gaiety, no, the life was too hard for that. Her mother was up at dawn each morning to feed the hens and stir the mash for the pigs, and the fire had to be lit, and the water fetched

. . . God, the life was hard enough without it being made unbearable.

'Stupid, stupid Eileen!'

Just when her mother must have thought that there was no lower to sink. She wanted them all to be kept decent, wanted it too badly. She remembered when they got the carpet over in McGurk's farm. Nice and soft it was under your feet. They took her mother inside, right into the parlour to show it off, and she came home all flushed with pleasure and hating the cold stones of their kitchen. She used to put flowers in empty jars. She had hopes for them, she ached for the touch of silk or soft cotton, fine woollens, surrounded as she was by hardness: the roughness of sacks in the barn, the tight twist of hemp, the course calico shifts they wore at night, patched and re-patched. She wept at the sight of the thick navy darning on their stockings, itchy and rough against chapped skin.

They used to sit around at night. Talking about what fine people they would be, wearing the best of everything, and never walking anywhere.

'McGurk's son had one of them motor cars, Nora,' she said. 'You can laugh now, but it was like a scene out of hell, breathing smoke, and the rattle as it went past. There were no roads out that way, just a few lanes and everyone for miles would come out to watch. Eileen went riding in it. I remember the car waiting at the bottom of the lower fields and my mother fussing over her. She was beautiful. They all said that no one for miles around could match her. She had long hair that my mother twisted up for her in two flat loops on either side of her head. She was a neat dancer, they said, with a quick, light step. But I remember her moving slowly, heavily, a solid woman. But she once had a neat waist, nipped in. My mother had dreams for that one. They said Eileen was like her.

'Listen, my mother filled her head up with notions. McGurk's put up the rent of the lower fields, where the best grazing was. Daddy couldn't pay. And they were just left . . . fallow.'

Her voice trailed off.

'Grandma . . . Listen, what do you think . . .?'

Nora was talking to her . . . what did she want . . .? what did it matter what she thought!

'We've been thinking about the name . . . we thought Eileen, after your sister, there's no one else in the family by that name . . . What do you think . . .?'

Sweet Jesus, protect us! The old woman began a novena in her head. Holy Mary, Mother of God, pray for us sinners, now and at the hour of our death. . . .

'What do you think!'

Holy Mary, Mother of God . . . perhaps when she finished praying it would be over and they would change their minds. She felt as if the worst kind of paralysis had gripped her. Slowly she forced words out. Her tongue was heavy and not ready to co-operate. She pretended she had not heard. Nora repeated it.

'Eileen we'll name her. What do you think?'

Good God Almighty. If she said what she thought, would they ever be happy again! She had to make them stop.

'Why not Eileesh?'

The old woman tried to smile . . . must let them think that it was nothing other than a preference. She sat still. For how long had she slept?

Suddenly she was seized with a spasm and she said aloud, 'The consequences . . .'

Nora's bright eyes were on her. She had not meant to talk her thoughts. They would have to bear the consequences. What could she do? She wagged her finger noiselessly and knew how Nora looked at her, and saw an old woman full of superstition. Dredging up history was dangerous; she intended taking it with her to the grave. Since her brother died six years ago, she alone carried the intolerable burden of guilt. She would not pass it now to anybody, it deserved to be buried finally. Nora was always so curious and bit by bit she had ravelled some of the story out of her; asking questions, following half-understood clues and messages.

Eileen was in limbo, as if she never existed. Nora did not deserve such a burden. But the innocent baby to be damned by that name. She rose from the chair holding a quavering finger out.

'You will have to bear the consequences then . . .' she said to her.

And he, great gombh, all he said was, 'I like the name. What's wrong with it?'

So dense he could not see that she was troubled. At least Nora shut him up.

'My grandmother's upset . . . you know there's always been a problem about my great-aunt . . . she was the one that was a bit touched . . . no one talks about her.'

'Oh God, you don't pass that down by giving someone the same name.'

The old woman wanted to spit on his answer. He thought he knew it all . . . he thought that she was worried because the little one might end up stupid. . . . God forbid . . . the only stupid one was himself.

Eileen had been turned, didn't they see that? No, they saw a superstitious old woman shaking and muttering. She sat down. Dignity, she thought. Maintain the silence of years . . . the silence of her father, ruined and hating . . . the guilty silence of her mother, silence following them to their graves, and Eileen after them, singing songs like a child. The family after this generation would have survived its massive fall from grace, it should be forgotten.

God give me the strength to keep my mouth. But she saw Nora's eyes, saw the curiosity in them and knew that she would watch and listen, even to her mutterings, just as she had learnt the truth by watching, picking up the scent of her sister. Her mother warned her brother never to talk of it. But she had listened and pieced it together, then she asked.

Hell broke loose, all the hate and shame spilled over, and when she knew for certain, she understood the need for secrecy.

She sat back against the wall. She had been too young to know half of what was going on. She was eight or nine. She shook her head. Why wouldn't they explain to her? Her sister's face stared at her; big, round, terrified eyes she had. There had been madness then; they drew it in with their breath. Disgrace too. There was no escape from it. And her own grandfather was dying in the back room, like she ought to be now. The adults were scared to mention it inside the house in case he heard before he died.

That was something she wanted Nora to know.

'You must always speak well of the dead, did you know that? Oh, aye. Their spirit will hear you out and take the bitter sound of any hate with it to the next world. It will fix upon their souls and deny them eternal life.'

There, it was said. Two stars fell for Eileen, two souls clinging together in death. Nora was looking at her. Had she said that out loud too?

Birds swarmed in the sky, long ago. They massed over the trees behind the house where she grew up. It began with a distant buzzing which grew louder, as more and more rooks appeared in the sky until the sound drowned out everything else, and the sky was lost behind a curtain of beating wings which smothered the dying light. When they dispersed, night was there, having crept up behind their feathery blackness. The jagged edge of wings fled, leaving a motionless sky, just as waves tossed in a storm become restful as they fold into an ocean of glass. That was her favourite time of day. At the first sounds she would rush out into the field and wait for the rooks to arrive. She would stare and stare at the last scraps of sky before it disappeared completely behind the humming wings. Her father said it was the sound of souls in limbo, knocking at the entrance to heaven. She used to lift up her arms, wanting to help push them through, and throw her weight against those gates. It was a time of day when she felt her own soul soar, when her soul reached upwards and she could touch the sky and almost feel what was beyond.

Her mother hated it. A dour woman who never laughed and said that life was purgatory. But there had been a time when the same woman used to put flowers in jam jars. Her mother would put her hands tight over her ears and run back indoors to block out the noise of the rooks screeching. She stopped going out at all, she would not put a foot on soil outside the back door. As evening approached and the rooks massed, someone always had to sit with her. She dreaded that time more than any other and would lose control of herself, screaming as she heard the wings beating on the roof. Her mother's eyes would stare up at the ceiling, her pupils wild and dilated. She said the house was full of whispering, a constant babble of sound, which built up to the dreadful crescendo of evening despair which battered upon her senses.

The old woman shrugged. She was irritated by the memory, angry with her mother who was always hearing things, because she never slept nights, always too busy listening to voices and unable to hear the living ones around her. Her mother stopped saying the rosary with them because all she could hear were voices which yelled above the sound of her prayers. She said she had no right praying; it was pointless trying to go on over their shouting and she was cut off, unable to communicate with her soul.

The old woman remembered her father, drunkenly swearing, screaming at his wife. He died first. It felt as if there was barely time enough for one body growing cold before the other sank down into the same hollows in the mattress, fitting into it, reoccupying the vacant space of death.

She jumped slightly, hearing a metallic crash, and saw Nora pick up a piece of coal that had fallen from the fire; carefully the young woman replaced it and laid the tongs back in the grate.

The dead, she thought, the dead. 'Never speak ill of them . . .' she muttered shaking her head from side to side. 'Never speak ill of the dead. . . .'

To Nora it was all mystery, the old woman spoke in riddles. Great aunt Eileen was the enigma. Dead before her own life started, her name seemed to haunt her childhood by its absence. Once or twice alluded to and then forgotten, as if she had no soul. Did any of them ever pray for her? Why could she not know? She knew very little about Eileen, only that something had gone terribly wrong, but what, she could not imagine. Nora had heard stories from other people, a very old neighbour remembered her great-aunt sitting at home all day playing with dolls. Nora wondered if she was mentally ill and that's what they had all been so ashamed about. Yet the neighbour told Nora that her mind had 'been destroyed'. That was the phrase he used; why 'destroyed'? She touched her grandmother's arm, she appeared to be sleeping.

The old woman felt the touch, but did not want to chance opening her eyes. She remembered that Eileen had seemed to will her own end. One day she just decided not to live any more so she died quietly indoors. She was buried next to her mother in the clearing just before the woods; away from the church these two lay, isolated even in death. No one passed comment on it now, everyone imagined that the priest had consecrated the ground, but the old woman knew he had not.

She knew there was a third grave, and she alone knew where it was. No one else discovered it. She could not tell her brothers. She only pieced the truth together after Eileen's death. But it was a fearsome secret to have kept.

Before she understood what had happened she thought her sister was crazy. A shuffling great imbecile who was touched in the head. She was ashamed. Everyone knew she was the sister of big, slow Eileen.

At home Eileen would suddenly up and walk out to the kitchen without a word. She would disappear for hours on end and their mother would scream that someone should have gone with her. Always needing watching, always needing protecting, that was her sister.

Being the youngest, she was usually sent to track her down and bring her back. She hated that. Everyone else was too busy and their mother no longer set a foot outside. The old woman remembered how she would tail her elder sister, not wanting to be seen by anyone. She would follow and keep watch from a distance, playing games along the way.

Eileen always walked to the furthest field. There was a small hill fort before the fencing and in the lower field six standing stones in a circle. The area was full of stone circles. No one thought them remarkable until lately. The old woman smiled, all their life they had standing stones in the fields and the cattle grazed around them, now they came out from the city and put plaques in the ground and people came and stared at them. But they were nothing special to the farmers. Eileen always went towards this group. She would kneel in the middle of the ring, nursing her doll and singing, occasionally crying, and once a mad, ringing laugh that chilled the young girl's heart, crouching behind the trees.

She hated the duty of following her sister; she hated that stone circle, it was as if all the sadness in the world gathered there. It was a grey desolate place, cold even in summer.

'They blackened their souls, blackened their souls; that's what the bible said. They were without the light of salvation.'

Her mother used to wake up in the night, choking.

'She felt hands around her neck, you see,' she whispered, telling the very crux of the strange relationship between mother and daughter. But Nora had not understood anything, she thought it was simply a nightmare.

'But me father couldn't quieten her. He used to take a lantern. 'Look' he'd say, showing her the light. 'Look, there's nothing there, there's no one in the room.'

'But she could see footprints in the quilt, she could feel the weight of her murderer pressing down. And he would shake out the covers, smooth them over her and tell her it was a dream. She never slept. She lay awake at night staring into the dark, listening.'

The old woman sat up. What had she said? If her mind started to ramble she would blurt it all out in one sentence. If only they would not use the name! That had unsettled her. She should warn them. But the only way was by talking, after so long keeping silent.

In her youth the old woman thought that her mother was the cruellest of women. She wanted to forget everything, but the events haunted her mind, repetitive and recurrent, forcing her to dwell on them. Over many years she considered those events, reconsidered as time lengthened and memory altered, while those who had seen kept silent and died.

The old woman did not know when it was that she started to feel sympathy, but her mother was dead before she understood how such cruelty had been forced upon the woman. For what sort of a mother would she have been if she was not seen to condemn such behaviour? What sort of a family were they if they did not care enough to be angry? And Christ knew they were angry; because everyone had the opportunity to look down on them, even common labourers could point their fingers at them.

'It runs in the family.'

'Waywardness.'

'Irreligion.'

'What sort of a home does their mother keep anyway? I've heard there isn't a holy picture on the walls at all. . . .'

The failing of Eileen was read in each of them. Everything they did was open for comment, every word they spoke open to interpretation, their every move scrutinized for signs of moral weakness. Like father, like son. Like mother, like daughter. From the same blood . . . bad blood

120

. . . they saw their sly eyes watching them, their talk ready to start again when their backs were turned.

Those her mother hated most were the pious ones who came to sympathize, gloating with condolences. They should have been grateful. If they had daughters they ought to have got down on their knees and kissed the ground for sparing them the ignominy. Her mother had to live the shame each day. She prayed then, yes, asking God for a spate of it, for a sudden upsurge of wickedness so that it should not have been her daughter only.

Her poor mother was terrified that the old one in the back would get to hear of it. Such a thing, to die with knowledge of the disgrace. Spare the dying. But that was long ago, the old one in the back passed peacefully and deafly. Now she was the old one, she had to set the record straight.

'There were some round here that couldn't speak my mother's name without cursing her for what she did. But none of it was her fault.'

She saw Nora looking at her hard. She was not sure if she had spoken out loud. She was confused. She heard her granddaughter say, 'Whose mother? Which Eileen . . .?' but she shook her head.

'I don't want the facts to be wrong . . . it wasn't her fault, you know, lots of people will tell you that it was. Tell Eileen that it wasn't my mother's fault . . .'

Had Nora heard her? How could Nora understand?

She felt tearful and stared at the flames, wanting to burn out the water in her eyes and let it turn to steam, so she opened them very wide. The flames blurred and doubled as she looked. When she was a child there were spirits in the fire. There was a game she used to play, throwing her bad angel up the chimney after the fire smoke. They told her that a good angel sat on her right shoulder and watched over her, but the one which sat on her left was from the devil, placed there to lead her into temptation. She was too young to know which was her right and which was her left. The game she played was to seize both angels firmly in her hands and imagine how they wriggled, then she would hurl both into the flames. She trusted that God would save the good one, but the other would burn horribly and not torment her. Whenever she misbehaved, she knew the devil had sent a new envoy to persuade her to sin.

Could Nora hear her?

'Be fair,' Daddy used to argue with Tom McGurk, but there was no arguing. Their men had insructions to chase our cows out whenever they wandered in. Och, it broke my mother to be always in their shadow.'

'Whose shadow?' Nora asked.

'Shadow,' the old woman mouthed, 'Shadow?'

She sat up, straightening her back as best she could.

'Listen! Can you hear me . . .?'

She was frightened now that she talked to herself. She no longer knew when she spoke and when she was silent. She wanted Nora to know that he was a good man.

'My father!' she shouted. 'I don't remember them having one cross word until this business with Eileen. Then the house was full of shouting. Nothing was ever the same after. It was Mam that suffered the worst. She carried the burden for the rest of her life. It wore her away. She tried to pretend nothing happened, she would not let anything touch her heart. She set her face and went coldly about her tasks.'

There were no more jam jars with flowers in them about the house. She saw herself, a running thing once, a happy child in a laughing house.

'Yes, we did laugh, I soared with rooks, did you know that? I touched heaven and came back, and one day all the hopes were dashed. I was too young to understand but I knew something had ended.'

The old woman sank back exhausted as if she would sleep. Instead she shouted, and the sound came from deep in her throat. She felt it.

'Listen!' she screamed.

She remembered how her mother had performed her duty like any married woman, and being a proper woman it was rightfully a torture to her. Like it was to her.

'Why must it be so. . .?'

The births were too frequent, and they were foul. God, the pain, and her left alone waiting for the neighbour woman to come round. And her mother had tried to warn her about that, let her see what married life was . . . but there was nothing else, under the eyes of God she would not be a nun.

'I became someone's wife. My heart weeps for you although you don't care.'

Her granddaughter . . . she talked about having three children.

'Do you believe you can control God's plan?'

She did not look at Nora. The world is changing too fast, she thought. Had she talked, what had she said?

She felt her hand being lifted. It had dropped by her side as she dozed and hung limply. Nora placed it back on her knee, that might stop the cramp at least. She was a good thoughtful girl, sometimes too thoughtful. Her brows were furrowed now. The old woman wondered how much she understood. She saw how she watched her. They must have seen that she was failing, noticed how she shook with effort sometimes after crossing the room. That was why she had to refuse all help, she did not want them to feel too closely her life's ebb. She knew that time was running out and she intended to let it go its full course and not be propped up as she had before. Why had God left her for so long without calling her to his bosom? Was it to test her endurance? See how long she could keep silent? Each day of late she doubted her resolution.

And now, this awful shock, to cry up the dead, give the name to the innocent.

Oh, Sweet Jesus, is it for this that I've been kept alive? Is this why I'm still here? Spare me, spare me.

'She forbade us to ever speak of it, you see.'

Why was Nora looking at her so strangely?

The room seemed dark. Hadn't they lit the gas? Who was that standing in the doorway? Sean? But he was dead. Sean never carried a gun. He was intended for the priesthood. The family were going up in the world; every farmer's ambition, one son a doctor, another a priest. Not Sean. Not Sean in the doorway. This wasn't the same room, it was bigger. Or was the old place biggest? Remember . . . remember. She pinched her arm. No difference, the man still stood in the doorway. Like her father had that night.

'He beat her. Our Sean heard the screams from the barn and said it wasn't right no matter what she had done. He would have been a priest but if there was anything in the family, they wouldn't take you. No seminary could accept him after that. And he still would not blame Eileen. Too good he was for the church, he was a saint and no mistake. All the good men have gone. Who's that in the doorway? Out looking for the fox that's eating your hens? You'll have to be quicker. Quick like Sean. His life was ruined by that slip of a thing that didn't know what day it was and still, he would not blame her.

'My father beat her. Me mother said it was all that she deserved and would not go out to put a stop to it. We heard the screams from the barn. He could have killed her then, I think he wanted to. He thought he might beat it out of her.

'They wouldn't let her back into the house . . . she had straw to lie on and they locked the door against her. It was a cold night. All winter I think they hoped that she would die. God, that's a cruel thing to say about your own parents, but I think it's what they wanted. I didn't understand at the time. No one explained anything at all. . . . I had to listen and watch and learn. I only knew then that they kept her like a dog, no, worse, for a dog might come in and warm itself. She was made to go round the back like a tinker and stand to eat her food out in the yard. If it was to shame her, it did more harm to me mother, for that was still her daughter standing mute with the big cow's eyes accusing her. Weren't they of the same bad blood, wasn't the guilt me mother's too, for Eileen was of her making?'

She felt salt tears on her face.

'I don't know where she went. We didn't hear her. She fended for herself. Along with the bogey woman she slipped away. She got past somehow. Like they all did; even Kitty O'Shea, to carry the rag-wrapped spirit of Parnell, creeping back in the dead of night, with the bundle in her arms.

'I saw her next morning. She walked in without a word. A freezing blast of air followed her, as if she brought some chilled horror that was still in her eyes. Her pretty hair was disgusting, lank and sticking to her crown, and her hands were filthy, her nails full of soil as if she'd dug herself out of a grave. The skin about her face was ghastly, colourless, only round her eyes, deep shadows with such fright behind them . . . she was motionless without the strength to breathe or let her heart beat. It was a corpse that was once my sister, that's how she looked, like someone who had returned from the dead.'

The old woman remembered how in the morning it couldn't be found. There was clay on Eileen's boots and she threw them from her. Good strong boots and she burnt them. Her mother was slapping her. 'What have you done? What have you done?'

'Eileen never spoke. They knew someone had helped her, she was never that strong. But she just stared ahead like somebody sleepwalking . . . and me father tramped the field all day listening for the sounds of crying. He came back and stood in the doorway shaking his head. Empty-handed. Walked all day looking for fresh soil, a newly dug pit and found nothing. He combed the barns. There was mud on his boots and my mother screamed at him, "Don't bring that earth into this house!"

'She hated the red clay that clung to shoes, she hated the feel of soil under her feet. She would not have mud in the house after that, but she'd mop the kitchen after he'd passed through.

'"Leave your boots outside," she'd yell, and it wasn't house-proud had her that way. She hated cold earth, she hated soil because it covered the one who had never been, and all the farm became a cemetery to her. Everywhere she looked, she saw the unmarked places where the lost souls lay. And she knew then that she belonged among them with Eileen.

'I used to wonder, I used to dream . . . nightmares . . . seeing her holding it down gently in a basin, I'm sure she'd be gentle, waiting until it stopped fluttering, until there were no more ripples on the water. I've seen her that many times in slow motion lift it out . . . breaking the surface into circles to part for the slippery child. I wondered if it would still be warm? I used to think about that. She must have held it to her before she spared it the life of pain that would have been its lot. I wondered if she nursed it before digging its grave. . . .

'They thought she might have left it along a track. I know she put it somewhere safe where the world would not touch it. With no cross, no mourning rites, still she would leave it lovingly. She knew where it was. She went back there. A special place. They ought to have known that she would not have given it over to a stranger to be brought up as the unpaid skivvy. That would not have been her way. Reminded daily about its unsanctified beginnings; better to drown a child than leave it to that. . . .

'Mother said all the blame was hers because she turned her out. She couldn't talk to anyone outside the family. Darkness surrounded her, and Eileen. My mother just wasted away. Eileen, well she sat in nursing a doll, singing wee songs to it.

'I saw her once laying the doll down in the middle of the stone circle. It was a game. She picked wild flowers and covered the doll's face, bits of sticks and grass until the doll was hidden from view. Eileen walked slowly round the circle talking all manner of nonsense. I laughed at the time because I thought that she looked like the priests when they pace the aisles in church, reading the lesson to themselves.

'My mother was right when she believed that the country-side was full of graves. It took me years to work out what Eileen was doing.

'I remembered the strange game she used to play. I never told a living soul. Eileen was dead. What was the point in opening another wound for my brothers to bear. Another dark sin for Sean to learn?

'Do you know I've never set foot in those fields since? I won't go near those standing stones; I never liked them when I was a child, even then they used to scare me. Desolate, desolate place, pagan they are, there's no godliness, no sanctuary. Just the souls of the damned, and the unknown and the cold earth that covers the ones who never existed. The earth swallows up its mistakes.'

The old woman felt that an icy hand had been placed upon her back. She shuddered so violently that she needed to catch her knees to steady herself, but she could not move. Her hand would not rise, but was leaden as if it belonged to someone else. She concentrated on moving it and felt exhausted from the effort. Slowly and heavily she placed it on her knee and was aware that she had lost all sensation in it. It lay curled like a claw. Time, at last. She saw the fields at home and herself skipping among them, heard her mother calling her in from the kitchen. A barn cat, black with green eyes, that she'd wanted to pet, ate scraps that she left at the door. Sean, studying in the corner by the lamp, the smell of tobacco from her daddy as she cuddled up for a goodnight kiss and she was being carried up the stairs warm with a big towel around her, warm from the tin bath in front of the fire. She peered out, down under the quilt and her mother singing, and she was smaller, and smaller, fading away from sight . . . the smell of bacon . . . and the old one sitting in a chair by the fire . . . 'Don't disturb your granda,' they'd whisper, 'he's frail.' What was frail? She danced at her wedding. White, and the kitchen at home cleared, a big wooden table and Bridget singing 'Dicey Riley, taken to the drink' and them all pioneers. Her father dead long ago, thank God, she'd be cooking him dinners still, not able to fend for himself. Four daughters she had, each one lovelier than the next, but widowed then. Four girls needed marrying off. God was giving her a hard time. Sitting at another wedding, the first one to marry, and not the eldest, that caused a stir . . . and grandchildren. Funerals. Where was Nora?

In front of her eyes the image of someone huddled in thought . . . a long way off. The fire had gone out. That person did not notice. She heard a shout, Nora was screaming. The old woman knew then that it was true. Everything she had said was true . . . and you should never speak ill of the dead, for the hearing was the last to go.

White Christmas, 1953

It was the time when she first gave birth that had hardened her against any sentiment. God, how she had suffered to bring their son into the world. And she had been terrified, left on her own in that miserable room; it didn't seem right, not on her first ever time. She had even begged that nasty nurse to stay out of desperation. That bitch!

'You are not the only woman to be having a baby,' she told her. 'I've got other younger women making less fuss than you!' and she flounced out, leaving Nell frightened and miserable, scolded like a schoolchild with tears beginning to well up in shame for her self-pitying nature. Then the pain would start again.

'Jesus, Mary and Joseph!' she screamed. 'Help me! Help me!'

But no one did. When a nurse finally came, it was to tell her off. She put her head round the door.

'Oh, stop shouting, you silly girl!' she said and withdrew.

Nell was crushed. Forty-one was too old to be having a first baby. Everyone had told her that and filled her with anxiety.

'Anything could go wrong,' her unmarried sister said, but no one told her what. She had gone in the first time expecting to die. She thought that was why they were leaving her alone.

He came in the day after, tired from work. Her eyes

stared emptily at him. She had touched depths of fear previously unknown and had been shocked. She felt resentful. What did he know? Him and his bloody work. She felt then as if she hated him. She blamed him. It hadn't been what she expected. They would not let her see the boy for two days. They said it would upset her. He was covered in bruises from where the doctor had clamped and pulled and pulled. The violence of it was horrifying, everyone shouting instructions at once, screaming at her as though she had done something bad. She felt castigated. She had been punished more than adequately. And soft lad at work, getting off scot free. Christ! Men had it easy, no doubt about it. If they felt a tenth of the pain, they would insist on all families stopping at one.

Nine days before Christmas she had given birth to her second child, a girl. She did not know it then, but this daughter was also to be her last. She was only aware of the cramps in her womb each time she put the baby to her breast and watched it suck urgently, as if it already sensed that this blissful state would be soon curtailed.

Jet black the little one's hair had been, long enough to cover the head as she emerged, wet and glossy, and puffed up with her mother's hormones.

Nell's sister, on her only visit to the hospital, had started laughing as soon as she saw the child. 'It's got a bust. Look!' she exclaimed, surveying the child's chest through the deep square neck of the regulation gown that had slipped off its shoulders. She was amused to see a tiny new-born one with such apparent maturity, rushing towards adulthood.

In two days, the hair had already begun to lighten and drop out and the swelling was subsiding. The red mottled face grew paler. The baby was changing overnight and Nell didn't always feel sure when she went into the nursery that she would select the right one; she couldn't stop herself from checking the name tag each time.

He had come in to visit on the same evening after the

child had been born and saw for the first time his tiny daughter.

'She's beautiful,' was all he managed to say as he saw the delicate feet kicking the air and watched her mouth trying to taste the world around it. He was speechless with genuine delight. Nell looked at his face.

Soft bugger, she thought. It was all a mystery to him – he could afford to be in awe – she was the one with the stitches. She did not have feelings left to marvel with, they had been pummelled out of her.

She watched his back now as he walked out of the ward. She knew that she would not see him again for a while. He was working nights and it was difficult to get to the hospital, and the strict visiting hours did not help.

The baby grunted. She lifted it over to the other side. Fifteen minutes each way. She kept a close watch on the clock. She did not like feeding, but it was only for the first few weeks so she could endure it. They told her the first time that she did not have enough milk and they must have seen plenty of mothers to know; besides, a bottle was more hygienic.

During the day she would lie on the bed staring around the ward. Everything was white: all the hospital linen, the bed covers, the shifts they brought her for the baby, even the little blanket she wrapped the child in. Only the walls were different. Painted just a fraction off white, they were a pale cream, but sometimes even they looked the same. Nell would stare as everything merged together without boundary or edge, limitless without borders: the walls, ceilings, sheets, beds, even the baby and herself. She thought she might be going mad. Even the sky, when she glimpsed it through the windows, was colourless, as if all blood had been drained from the day.

She continued to bleed heavily. She wondered when it would stop. But it was all that broke the monotony, the occasional cluster of red stains on the sheets when the nurses came to change the bed.

She had been there nearly five days when they came to tell her she was being moved.

'Get your things,' the staff nurse told her.

'Am I going into another ward?'

All around her women were packing small toilet bags, equally unprepared. They had been told to send their suitcases home the first night.

'There isn't room to keep that,' the ward sister had told Nell when she arrived at the labour ward on the arm of the ambulance driver. 'Where is your husband? Out in the corridor? You will have to give it to him to take home.'

Nell was writhing as the stonger surges of pain gripped her. The ward sister was angry because Nell did not have a husband conveniently waiting in the corridor who could take care of everything.

'He's working nights, it's the shift,' she tried to explain, but the woman had towered over Nell, making her feel stupid and terribly wrong. She was scared to argue or say anything. The one time she had asked for help she had been shouted at; it made her wonder if any demands in hospital were unreasonable. She did not want to be a trouble maker, and hadn't the midwife scolded her for making too much fuss?

'You're being moved to Southport,' the nurse at the desk informed her. 'Sign here. It's just a formality. Have you got everything?'

Nell carried a brown paper bag in one hand, containing a tube of toothpaste, a comb and some hair curlers. Her hair was an irritation, fine, sparse and grey, she put rinses in to keep it brown, but the roots must have come through by now because she had not done it for weeks, but it was the least of her worries.

'Why am I being moved?'

The nurse looked up from writing, surprised to see that Nell was still there. 'You're not the only one,' she said continuing to write.

'I can see that, but why are we being moved?'

'Overcrowding. We're expecting ten new admissions this weekend. We need the beds. You're being sent to a nursing home.'

Later that morning Nell was bundled up and the baby brought out of the nursery and given her to hold. It was the longest time she had nursed her child as she was pushed along lying on a trolley, staring up at the ceiling, feeling disorientated. How would he know where she was? Nobody in her street had a telephone, not even the corner shop, and when they asked her if she knew his work number she thought they meant his national insurance at first. She could not even remember the name of the factory he had been sent to that week.

'Never mind, we'll tell him on his next visit,' they said brightly, as she was called. But when would that be? Two, three days? She felt unnerved. Her sister had come over from Ireland, but she was busy looking after Nell's son while her husband worked. She could hardly get in in the evenings. They would not allow children in the wards and the boy was too small to be left on his own outside. But if it was not awkward enough already, how would Joe ever get to see her in Southport?

He'd have to get the train from Exchange Station, and a bus, two buses, one either side. It would take him hours and he would not be able to stay, on account of getting all that way back again. It would be impossible for him to come, and unreasonable for her to expect it. She felt lonely already. It would be days before anyone knew where she was. He would only find out on his next visit and between then she would be out in Southport without a living soul knowing her whereabouts. It was a frightening thought.

Suppose something happened to him at work, suppose the police came to the hospital? She did not trust the nurses to remember who she was, or to give the correct information. Maybe she could write to him, save him the shock of turning up and seeing another woman in the bed. But she would need pen and paper and a stamp. Could she get them in the nursing home? Her mind raced with anxiety. She could always give the letter to a visitor to post; not the staff, if they were anything like this place they would just forget. She would look for someone sympathetic and go up and explain that she had just been moved.

She relaxed her grip on the baby and breathed a little easier now that at least she had a plan.

At the end of the corridor Nell was lifted up and put on a stretcher, a heavy blanket placed over her, and she was carried outside. She felt powerless.

'Hang on a minute, love' one of the bearers said as they gently laid the stretcher down on the firm snow beside the ambulance. They said something to her, but she did not catch it. All she heard was the soft thud as the stretcher touched snow, and she knew that she was alone. The men had left her to look for something, keys or a watch. She lay cuddling her baby under the blanket, staring at the winter's sky and people's feet as they passed her in the hospital grounds. It was a strange view of the world. She felt very small, dwarfed by life around her until she looked down and saw her tiny child.

The temperature had dropped, cold enough for snow, it felt like it would feeze. Overnight the roofs would ice up and pipes burst in homes all over Liverpool. She held the baby close to her to retain body heat, beginning to feel scared in case she had been abandoned, left on her back with a five-day-old baby. She could see the headlines already. 'Irish woman found frozen to death outisde Liverpool Hospital. New baby in intensive care machine. Horrified father says he was working nights.'

She wrapped her arms tighter about the tiny thing so that it might not feel the cold. Nell was worried that the baby would become ill and she squeezed it to herself in panic.

'If anything happens to this child, trouble-maker or not, I'll go back in there and strangle the nurse with my own

134

bare hands, the one that made me sign the form. See if I don't!'

When she looked around for signs of the men returning, all she could see was the cold, clean, clinical snow. White. She was entombed in it. Only the path showed through, a living trail of black asphalt. Snow began to fall again, she was aware of it tickling her face, then dampening her hair. She watched the baby licking snowflakes with its new pink tongue and for one giddy moment felt herself sinking as if she had just come to the end of a fall, when the weight of her body would jar in her knees, as she struggled to stay upright. But she was not upright, she was lying down, or had been. The ground under her was spinning. Thank God for the snow on it, at least it would be soft to fall in. But she did not fall. She pushed the baby down under the blanket so that its face was protected and clasped the little white bonnet tightly to its head. The few wisps of dark hair escaping from it were like slashes, deep, dark and shocking. She focused all her attention on her child's black hair. The white sky was moving again. She felt her sense of balance being upset, so she concentrated on her daughter's safety. It took her a long time to realize that the men had returned and it was they who must have lifted her. She was back inside the ambulance and could not remember getting there. She heard the engine warming up and the slow movement of the wheels as they turned down the drive. All the way to Southport she lay on her back where they had placed her. She could not see out. The baby slept and, lulled by the sound of the engine, Nell dozed.

She was lonelier than she had ever been in Southport. No one came to visit her. They recommended after the birth that she stay in for two weeks, which was normal practice and she knew that he would not be able to come on Christmas Day because there was no transport. If she had been in Liverpool he would have walked into the hospital or taken a taxi, but all the way to Southport, that was a different matter. Maybe her sister would come on Christmas Eve, but that would mean leaving Brendan with a neighbour and it would be awkward.

She missed her little son all the more for knowing that she would not be able to see him. She felt sorry for her husband too, rushed off his feet all the time, having to leave his son with someone so he could get out to work. It was good of Bridget to offer to stay with them and help them through this time, but Nell was worried because her husband never liked Bridget, and she could imagine the atmosphere at home.

Bridget held him responsible. He made Nell go through all this a second time when the first birth had almost killed her. Bridget said that men were pigs. Older than Nell, she was unmarried. She had no time for men and physical contact with them, sex, was horrific to her. To Nell it was not much better, but it was no longer a mystery. She had the knowledge which struck terror into Bridget's wild imagination. The sisters would have been ashamed to speak to each other about such matters and Nell felt sullied in her sister's gaze.

They had gone down to meet her at the Pier Head, Nell large and cumbersome, slowly following Joe. He had been the one to spot Bridget out of the crowds pouring down the gang plank.

'Stand back against the wall,' he shouted to his wife. 'Stay by the gates, we'll come out to you.'

There was such a crush she could easily get hurt. She stood back and then she saw them coming up over the cobbled stones where the buses picked up passengers for Lime Street. Joe was carrying Bridget's suitcase and Nell could see that neither spoke to the other as they walked stiffly along, without pleasantries to take the edge off their meeting.

Nell had not wanted to wait outside, for it allowed her sister to scrutinize her from such a length. She wanted to be on top of her so that Bridget would not have time to stare at her disgusting belly. She felt coarse, red-faced and common. Bridget was slim. Always had been. Her hair was still dark and thick, and she had put it up in a roll on the back of her head. She looked strict and efficient, like a schoolteacher.

She knew that Joe would be having a harder time under Bridget's cold stare. This time Bridget had an air of contempt about her, letting Nell know that she only had herself to blame. Bridget disapproved of their marriage right from the start and, being the eldest, had a right to say so. She was fond of airing her opinions. She could do so without words, just a look, a gesture of hopelessness towards Joe, and he would understand and be awkward and wary in his own home. It was not right. Nell's eyes felt hot. She so wanted them to be together this Christmas; it was her family, she was a mother with two children now and a husband. Her sister did not fit into any of her calculations, she was the visitor who came among them and made them nervous.

She had not wanted it to be like this. She thought Christmas would be lovely this year with a new baby, but the practical matters had stopped any celebrating, keeping her prisoner and trapping him. It was not right. In her arms she held what was to be the most precious Christmas present ever. She wanted to give him his daughter on Christmas Day; her gift. It had, after all, been worth it and this little one had been so eager to be born, not like the boy who hung back timidly, reluctant to explore. He wanted the certainty of her womb; unlike this one who had hardly given her time to count between contractions, the pain coming so fast, and suddenly she was there yelling, still in a hurry.

Joe could not get out to Southport so he had sent her a pound note to buy things she might need. She spent it on women's magazines and bars of chocolate from the counter in the foyer. She never spent money on herself like this, she was thrifty through necessity and would not dream of wasting it, but she felt desperate for comfort and each time she parted with a coin, a little shiver of excitement ran up her back. She had spent a whole half-crown one day and could not stop herself from grinning as she scurried back to the small ward with the other nursing mothers. There were times when it felt as though it was part of a strange holiday that she had not chosen for herself.

He sent her a Christmas card. When she opened it a five pound note fluttered out. She stared at it in amazement. He must have been feeling rotten. She had an idea.

'Get yourself something,' he had written inside. She decided to get a taxi.

She was supposed to stay in for six more days, it was usual, but she felt fine and the baby was healthy. She reasoned that if she had given birth at home no one would have made her go away for two weeks. The two weeks was supposed to build her up; solid food placed in front of her, more meat than she had ever seen, and a warm dry nursery for the baby. When she thought about the damp at home her resolve wavered; was she being selfish wanting to rush the baby out of comfort and let it discover early that she had not been born with anything remotely resembling a silver spoon?

It was Christmas Eve. Nell stood in the entrance hall with a brown paper carrier bag.

'I don't care,' she told the charge nurse that morning, 'I'm going home and that's that. He can't get up here for Christmas and by the time I write to him asking for my clothes the holiday will be over. I'll go the way I am. Please, I want to be home for Christmas.'

She stood in the hall wearing her overcoat over her nightdress. She did not have a dressing-gown and for the first time she was glad of the fact.

'I understand,' the nurse said to her. 'Just sign here will you, it's an acknowledgement of your responsibility.

Nothing important, just a formality,' and she smiled. Nell was sure that it was the first time she had seen one of them smile.

As she waited in the entrance a group of junior nurses walked past. One shouted back to her, 'Have a lovely Christmas,' and Nell noticed how their eyes became strangely glassy as they saw her standing with her baby. Christmas was after all a time for families.

Behind Nell the holy family stood in tableau. The ass's head which peeped out from behind a holy man genuflecting, was nothing more than a head cleverly stuck into a block of wood, so that viewed from the front it appeared to be a complete animal. The committee which had donated the crib had managed as best they could with limited resources. Nell thought that it was lovely. The Christ child lay in an orange box with bits of straw strewn around to make it look authentic, although the words 'first grade tomatoes' appeared down the side of the make-shift manger. Supposed to be the image of life, the statue was heavy and lifeless. Its over-plump arms were modelled into wrinkles which were no longer desirable in a child. Paint flaked from them. It looked convincing enough to Nell, it made her shudder, especially when icy blasts from the entrance door blew across its bare torso.

A group of schoolchildren were doing the rounds singing carols in the wards. Their high voices reached out into the corridor.

> 'Hark the herald angels sing
> Glory to the new-born king.
> Peace on earth and mercy mild
> Christ and sinners reconciled.
> Hark the herald angels sing
> Glory to the new born king.'

It rang in her head, playing over and over all the way back in the taxi. She knew that she was being reckless. She tried not to look at the meter as it ticked away. It stood at three and six before they had even left the nursing home grounds. Christmas rates! There was no way of stopping the machine and little point in making herself anxious about it. She stared at the meter, hating it and hoping to put it off, but it coolly registered another sixpence. She ignored it. The Christmas spirit was taking her over.

Glory to the new-born king!

She clutched her own new-born child to her and loved it angrily. She was part of the Christmas message, hers was the model holy family. She felt that she could have run all the way back to Liverpool or flown on the feathery wings of the herald angels.

She put her key in the door. All the way home she had anticipated his reaction. She was going to wish him happy Christmas and give him his daughter to hold. He might even cry. She would turn away, she would not mind. They would both stay up late together after Bridget had gone to sleep and fill their son's stocking for Christmas morning, Bridget would have made sure that there was plenty of small things for that, and the baby would sleep in her own little cot for the first time. It was going to be lovely. She turned the key and pushed the door open. The house was silent. Bridget must have taken the boy out. She was late bringing him back, but Nell was not worried, Bridget would have him warmly wrapped up against the weather. She stepped inside.

Something felt different. She smelt paint. She sniffed. Fresh paint, he must have been redecorating as a surprise. No wonder he'd been tired when he came to the maternity hospital the first time. He must be getting one of the rooms ready, she thought delightedly. At last they would have another bedroom and they would move their son into it and let the baby sleep at the foot of their bed. They would not all have to sleep in the same room. Maybe he had got the damp looked at, maybe he'd paid someone to replace the floor boards after all. But behind the paint there was a fusty smell of old damp that she knew too well. The smell of mould underlying everything. In one breath she took it all in, the rotting wood upstairs, damp, dust and fresh paint. But something was not right, she felt it. There was too much paint for one thing, it was overpowering, and the house was too quiet.

She walked slowly up the dark lobby and flicked on the light switch, its click announcing her like an intruder in the still house. Where was everybody? It felt very cold. Under the kitchen door came a chilling draught which caught her ankles, ludicrous in fur slippers. She pulled her coat around her; the thin nightdress underneath made her feel naked. She was scared. If she opened the door and went into the kitchen she would see everything. She stood without moving. There was still time. She could creep back out through the front door and bolt away down the street before she had made any discovery. But what would she do? Go back to the nursing home? They would not take her back; she had signed a form, and anyway, one of the neighbours might see her and wonder what she was up to in her nightdress. With brooding anticipation she knew that she had to stay. She edged the kitchen door open and peered around.

As far as she could see, everything was white. She could not believe it. White paint dripped out of an empty tin hanging upside down from a ladder. The lino was covered with splashes spreading from the centre like a giant white chrysanthemum which unfolded its snowy petals as the paint spread across the floor. A plank was balanced across two ladders, while another had come unhitched and lay half-propped up against the wall. A piece of sandy tarpaulin was drenched in emulsion and lay discarded. White had splattered up the walls; and the settee, which he had not covered, was ruined. The rest of the furniture he had bundled into one corner and thrown a sheet over, but she saw how the chair legs which protruded had been sprayed.

Nell stared; there was so much white, she thought that she was back lying in the snow. She began to reel with horror and caught the wall with one free hand to steady herself. Her palm was coated in the emulsion. She opened her mouth to scream and saw the back door suddenly blow open. Joe stood there in the cold wiping paint off himself with a rag. He bent down and began to heave a bucket of water up the steps. It splashed, soaking his feet. He was cleaning up the catastrophe. As he looked up he saw her and froze. His carefully planned surprise had backfired.

Nell stood there stupidly, her eyes round with dismay, she looked as though she might cry. That would be the final insult to him; that she should turn up unexpectedly and blame him for not being prepared. He crashed his paint brush down on the yard step and swore at her. He had a foul temper when things did not go according to plan. He blamed everyone else for things which went wrong. If only they would leave him to himself, he used to say. Then he could get things done, finish jobs, without all this bloody interference. He could never get to the end of a job in peace. He was sick of it, he had put up with a week of her bloody sister, he was not going to let her start on him after that.

'Why the bloody hell couldn't you have stayed in for another week!' he yelled.

For a second, her eyes met his and he saw and recognized in them that strange, empty look he had seen once before and never been able to forget. That look with which she greeted him on the birth of their first child; when, in the moment before she stared past him as if he was not there, she had fixed on him a glance of total condemnation, before dismissing him from her life for good. Now Nell was staring past him again, her eyes empty. She felt her heart blanch as all feeling in her turned away from him. All feeling, for he had hurt her in a way that she could not understand and once again she was shocked by the force of her suffering. The baby, aware of nothing but its own hunger, began to cry.

Oblivious as a Roundabout

'Never mind, love, you're still young, there will be others,' said the woman. She reached out and took the younger woman's hand in her own, and at the same time seated herself on the hospital bed with her coat spread out around her. Her bag fell to the ground. She did not notice.

'I know it must feel awful now but you will get over it, like I did.'

Between her own soft palms, Theresa felt the roughness of the hand, with callouses bequeathed by a lifetime of hard work. It had given its best years and now wore faint brown age spots like tiny medals. The finger joints were swollen and the ring finger bulbous from the gold band tightening over the passage of time. Large and heavy, yet its touch was surprisingly gentle. Theresa shrugged and looked up at her mother-in-law.

'I don't know.' She was wary.

'Oh, of course there will.'

'I expect so,' but Theresa's voice was without enthusiasm.

'I thought the doctor said you could try again in a few months?'

Theresa nodded.

'Well, that's not so bad, is it?'

But Theresa could imagine the months stretching ahead bleakly – it would just be empty time that did not count, all that mattered was the result at the end of it, whether she could manage to get through the gestating period successfully. She saw herself as a hatcher of eggs. An incubator waiting to learn if she could keep a tiny thing that might grow into a life. Tears began to collect in her eyes and she could not stop them. Not now, she thought, not in front of his mother and his Auntie Sal.

'You have a good cry, girl, it will do you good,' said a second woman who had remained standing throughout. Theresa cried with her head down in her arms. She did not look at either of them and she did not hear them, until a voice told her it was leaving some things. But visiting could not be over already, or had she sat for so long with her head down without realizing? She looked up and saw the standing woman stacking things up on the bedside table.

'I'll just put these things here, girl; there's some grapes, and biscuits, and a couple of blocks of chocolate, that's for energy. They don't give you much room, do they?'

The seated woman spoke. 'Look here, Sal, they don't expect you to bring a week's groceries with you when you're admitted. They will feed our Theresa, you know.'

'Oh, I dare say, but hospital food's rotten.' She continued to pull things from a string shopping bag.

'There's some cold meat, ham and liver sausage, and a quarter of luncheon meat: I wasn't sure whether you liked that . . . and I got you a few crusty rolls. Oh, and I nearly forgot . . .' her hand plunged to the bottom of the bag. 'I got you one of those malted energy plus drinks, if you feel you can't manage much.'

Over her arm, Theresa saw two nurses stop in disbelief. They watched the busy woman from the other side of the ward. Despite herself, Theresa laughed.

Unaware, the woman continued to sort out packets and brown paper bags.

'You know when my old feller went in for the hernia, his blood pressure shot up something terrible,' she said. 'They put him on this salt-free diet, and he nearly drove me mad asking for cheese and onion crisps and pork pies every time I went near him. . . . Shall I put this fruit over here away from the window so it doesn't spoil?'

Her hands were busy rearranging the small table top. The other woman nodded as if she did not much care.

'He told me he was starving, all he did was complain. Glad to see me? You'd never have guessed it. . . . I took him a dozen hard-boiled eggs one night and you should have heard the things he called me! I couldn't stand it in the end. I smuggled him one of those Melton Mowbray pies, you know, the catering-sized ones. It's supposed to do about sixteen people. I said to him, "If you burst the pressure gauge when they come around tomorrow, you've only got yourself to blame."'

The other woman nodded slowly. 'Well, hospital food isn't to everyone's liking, is it? Do you remember when I had the cyst removed? There was a woman next bed to me, her husband used to bring her these cold bacon butties wrapped in a dishcloth. Everyone else got flowers.'

It hurt Theresa to laugh. She was still very weak. Food made her feel ill. She would get a nurse to take it all away as soon as they were both gone. The smell of liver pâté was disgusting. But life had to go on. She would have to get back among them soon, she just wanted a little time to mourn, that was all. She did not want to plunge back to normality too quickly, she wanted to return a bit warily this time.

Her visitors were talking across beds, to a middle-aged woman who had come to see the elderly patient next to Theresa. The white-haired woman stared past, forgotten, a solitary get-well-card on her table.

Theresa was lucky, everyone had been extra kind to her. It was times like this that she enjoyed the closeness of his family and the way they had accepted her into it. Her parents were dead and her brothers had both emigrated, so she was alone, in a sense. His family had all sent her something: cards, little messages, to let her know that they were thinking about her. His brother had even sent a huge bunch of flowers in on the first night, when it was still touch and go, no one certain what would happen or whether the baby was going to be all right.

They had fallen over each other in their haste to get to her and be the first to say that they knew what it felt like. It was almost as if she had joined a club, and she was shocked by it at first, like being elected to an elite confraternity. Didn't they have names for those things in America? Her brothers would know. Sororities? Womboratory. United in failure, the women looked at her.

'I lost two, you know,' her mother-in-law said. 'But I didn't let it stop me. I went on and had five. It won't stop you.'

'Lots of women lose the first one and don't even know about it . . . they don't have time to discover that they're pregnant because it's all over so quickly,' Auntie Sal told the next bed's visitor.

'Well then, that's the easiest way,' the visitor replied. 'Not that I'd know anything about it, I never married.'

'By God, but you're a sensible woman. Did you hear that?'

'I did,' Theresa's mother-in-law shouted across the side, 'and sometimes I wish I never had.'

'That goes for me too,' Sal grinned. 'All that effort and for what?' She began to laugh. The nurses giggled as they returned to their work. Theresa shook her head in mock disbelief, and the visitor looked at the white-haired woman she had come to see.

'Where does it get you in the end?' she said, while the old woman stared ahead without comprehending. Raising her voice, she leaned towards the patient. 'I said, Mother . . . Where does it get you. . .?' But she could not make the effort to repeat the whole sentence.

'Oh, never mind,' she ended irritably, used to a lifetime of monologues.

The old woman's mouth worked steadily, her jaw never

still, as she pushed her false teeth in and out of place and chewed on nothing.

Surrounded by all these warnings, Theresa wondered why she had been so excited to be pregnant. She had felt delighted by the prospect of motherhood. She loved the idea and felt wonderfully, deliciously purposeful. Her husband told her that her eyes shone.

They were both stupidly happy, like children; for eleven weeks. Until she felt the sharp pain in her belly which doubled her up, gasping for air. Between spasms of pain she limped next door to use the phone. The woman took one look at her and made her lie down. Her husband rang an ambulance and then John at work. By the time he had cleared it with the manager and clocked off, she was already on her way to hospital with a threatened miscarriage.

'Try not to move. Lie flat on your back,' the stretcher bearer told her. She tried to do as he said, but the pains were coming faster. She drew her knees up in agony and wondered if that had been the trigger, because that was when she felt the bleeding start. It flowed steadily all the way to hospital.

When she recovered consciousness, John was sitting beside her, looking older and tired. She was wearing a starched nightdress that was not hers.

'We have lost our baby,' was what he said. He wanted to get her quickly to the point of acceptance.

She screamed. 'Is there nothing left?'

He shook his head.

'I just want you better,' and he buried his head in her lap to cry.

She did not understand then, but it was with relief he cried. She had been so pale and ill that he thought he might lose her as well. It terrified him to see her so weak.

He knew that she was the stronger of the two, he was the one who would not be able to go on without the other. Once they had played, asking each other what they would do if one of them were to die, and he had said that he wanted to go first. She told him that was selfish, and asked, what about her? Then she had laughed that strong, clear laugh she had, throwing back her head. But he had meant it.

'The doctor told me that you will be back to normal soon,' he said, looking up.

She had no idea what that meant.

'Just move your feet up a bit, love. . . .' It was Auntie Sal feeling the mattress for springs. She kneaded the blue quilted stuff with her fist.

'These beds get some use.' Her fist punched and bounced. 'I knew it! There's a dip in this.'

The bell for the end of visiting had sounded twice when the nurses came round clearing people away from beds. Theresa might have known her visitors would be the last to go. Auntie Sal had not heard it at all.

'We'll have to go,' her mother-in-law said, urgency beginning to sound in her voice.

'Here's the ward sister. Leave that, Sal, for God's sake,' and turning to the nurse she smiled. 'Well, I expect you've got work to do. You don't want us cluttering up the ward.'

'It's long past visiting,' the uniformed woman said humourlessly.

'Don't you have any better beds?' Sal asked, straightening up stiffly. She rubbed the small of her back with her fist. 'A bad mattress can do terrible damage when you're bad with your back like I am.'

'Sal, come on, Theresa's not in with her back. . . .'

The nurse did not answer, but took her fob watch in her left hand and studied it carefully. Theresa, fearing that Sal might bring a mattress in with her next visit, made the effort to perk up. She sat upright,

'This bed is fine for me, I'm getting plenty of rest. Thanks for coming.'

She said the last so decisively that Sal proffered her cheek for a kiss automatically. The nurse walked on.

'We'll be in again,' her mother-in-law said.

Theresa watched the two women walk the length of the ward, their shoes clicking on the polished linoleum. She had meant it when she thanked them for coming in. Any distractions were welcome. People, hospital routine, anything that stopped her brooding. That was why she dreaded the night. Lying awake while the nightmare came back, not waiting for sleep. If she dozed, however lightly, it broke through the surface of her dreams, and it submerged itself like a drowning man just beneath the surface of her waking.

That evening, after tea was over and they clattered back to their beds, she sat up, not reading the book she held, but wondering why that memory haunted her. John knew the whole history. She had made a point of telling him about the episode in her life. She did not want anything to come between them, facts freshly dowsed, intriguing because of their miraculous detection. She wanted no awful secrets, but the truth out in daylight, long known and commonplace.

John accepted everything. He imagined the horror as she described it. 'You poor bloody kid,' he had said, forgetting that it was a long time ago. 'If only I could have been there to help you, give you some support.'

'It was something I had to do alone. . . . That's just the way it was.'

In the hospital bed she hung her head so that the nurses might not see, but she clenched her fists tightly under the covers. Her jaw and neck were taut, the sinews like wire rods.

'I must not think about it, I do not want to think about it. I will not think about it.'

It was a litany that ran through her head and like most prayers she had ever offered, as useless. She kept seeing

149

herself as she had been ten years ago, younger, and on one occasion, careless.

'You were a fool,' she told her former self. 'A totally stupid fool!'

She was nineteen, skinny with a penchant for black clothes. Her skin was unusually pale, in some lights translucent. She wore her dark hair in a single thick plait that reached almost to her waist, a plait whose heaviness tugged at her forehead so that her eyebrows were pulled back and seemed to be always raised in surprise. She looked more innocent than she was. She knew she was good looking; someone always wanted to take her out and she was never left standing on her own for long at parties. Despite that, she was awkward with the opposite sex. She did not understand her feelings. One minute she would be talking normally, the next she would find herself staring at someone's mouth wondering what they would be like to kiss. She fell in and out of love, had crushes on the oddest people. It was a surprise to her the way her emotions behaved, and during a period she felt like an animal on heat. In her fantasies she had no rest, she was hot with lust. These were the times she became a woman who could jump on any man who looked at her twice. In reality she started going out with Mac. It was obvious that he fancied her, the way he kept dancing with her at the party and he hung around her all night. She felt hot and dangerous, randy and bleeding.

'Why not?' she thought. He was very good looking, it was time some of her fantasies became real, time to find out what sex was all about. She was great at foreplay. They went outside and kissed on the stairs and she felt her whole body melt deliciously. His hands explored her neck and ran up and down her back

'You're beautiful,' he said as he kissed her over and over. 'Can I see you tomorrow?'

Not half, she thought.

They went out together for a while and it was good and

exciting at first. She loved the sex. She felt contented. It did not last. Who first said that familiarity bred contempt? Some spark went out of the relationship. It was as if once they had worked their mutual desire out of their systems, there was no other reason to continue, but they did, out of habit. It all became dull and predictable, as her reason for him disappeared. But something had taken root in him – power, strength; she did not know what to call it. He sensed a hazy domination and was not prepared to have it wrested from him without a fight. Passionate clinches gave way to phone calls whose sole passion was jealousy; it was vicious and suffocating. He suspected her.

'Where were you?' he would ask and she could not understand it. When they were together he seemed to be contemptuous of her, but when she was out of his sight, he spent all his time checking where she was. He even started ringing her up at work to make sure she had gone in.

'Don't be such an idiot!' she would say to him. 'This phone could be tapped, do you realize that? This is a local government office.'

That had been a job she really enjoyed. She had happy memories of working there. It was her first step up and out of the rut she was in after leaving school. Why couldn't she think about that? Instead, she kept seeing herself in her lunch-break that awful day, standing open-mouthed in the chemist's round the corner from the office.

'Are you sure?' she asked the assistant.

'Well, the test was positive. I suggest you get yourself to your doctor for confirmation, if that's what you want.'

The assistant was about the same age as her mother would have been then. Theresa remembered that the woman had watched her with sympathy. Theresa did look younger than she was. Right then she felt scared. In her mind there was no question about what she would do, she knew she could not keep it.

She told Mac that she was pregnant. She expected him

to be sympathetic. She met him in the park during such another lunch-break, having spent the night wondering how to tell him – she already knew what she was going to do.

'There's something I need to discuss with you.'

'Yeah, what?'

She yawned. 'I've been up all night.'

His eyes flashed jealousy. 'What the hell have you been doing?'

'Worrying.'

He looked at her angrily.

'I'm pregnant.'

There was a small silence. She wondered if she should tell him that she had already decided, but left saying anything. She thought that he would see the impossibility of her position. He did, but not in the way she expected. He yelled at her.

'You fucking stupid whore! Why can't you be on the pill like all normal women. You have to be so different, think you know what you're doing, think you know better than anyone else; well, you're not so smart, Miss fucking know all; clever bitches like you can still get caught out!'

He relished the prospect of her pregnant against her will, revelled in the idea of her being 'caught out'. He made it sound like a game. He was violent, his face contorted with anger.

'You stupid useless moron! You bloody idiot! How could you be so thick?'

She was stunned, especially when his hand came down across her face and she felt the force of the blow. Her cheek stung. She said nothing. He turned away from her. She stared at his profile, hating it. She watched his chest heave and she hated the anger that forced his breath out in shuddery jerking gasps. All the time he muttered abuse under his breath.

'Thanks,' she said, 'I knew you would understand.'

He swung round and in a frenzy, hit her back and forth across the face.

'You filthy little tart,' he spat, and strode off.

Theresa stayed in the park for hours after, unable to return to work. It started to rain. She walked in circles. She watched some young boys playing on the heavy roundabout in the swing park. Truants who met up and passed the school day anywhere, unable to return home before half past four. Young and already practised in the art of deception. The irony of it made her laugh. All the time Mac had accused her of lying to him, always suspicioius, now he probably wanted to believe that it was someone else's child. He would be able to convince himself if he thought about it for long enough.

She sat on the damp grass while the fine rain saturated everything, but she was as oblivious to it as the boys on the roundabout. She was mesmerized by them, a blur of motion and colour. They were going too fast. She turned away, not wanting to witness accidents. The trees behind had turned into a smudge of brown and russet because she was crying.

She had not heard from Mac for over a week when he appeared one day, waiting outside her office. He said that it had been a great shock and asked her to excuse him for his behaviour.

'I behaved completely out of character.'

But Theresa wondered how long this new imposter might last.

'I don't have anything to say to you,' she told him, feeling her body stiffen as the urge to run swept over her.

'Look, just talk to me.' He walked alongside her. He had been drinking.

'Just a few whiskeys,' he said. He was sentimental. She felt nauseated listening to him talk. She did not forget that he had called her a stupid whore, a clever bitch who deserved to get caught, while he mouthed empty words now about love and commitment. Then she understood his change of heart and fear spread through her body. It would be his way of trapping her for good. He would be able to keep an eye on her all right with her at home looking after a baby.

'You'll make a lovely mum,' he said, stroking the ends of her hair so that a shudder of revulsion went down her back. Already he had turned her into 'lovely mum'. Let him tattoo that on his arm with a heart and a rose, MUM, in bloody letters. She told him to get lost. He put his hand out and seized her shoulder, forcing her to stop.

'I'll go straight round to your house and tell your parents.'

His face sneered, the soft look of hearts and roses had vanished completely. So that was it. Play along with me or else. She knew there was no escape from his maliciousness and she had to handle this carefully. For the first time she was going to lie to him. He had cornered her. So she kept up a pretence. She forced a grin, lopsided as an idiot's, and tried not to look at him.

'I knew you'd be pleased.'

She arranged everything in secret and kept meeting him during the evening after work. He grew stupid and sentimental, imagining her the mother of his child, living with her parents, and he would come visiting on the bus, proud of his virility. She used to retch after he kissed her. He thought it was the morning sickness. She said it was indigestion because her body was all out of sorts, and he agreed.

'Of course, of course,' he beamed, 'there's all sorts of miracles taking place inside you,' and he would pat her on the belly, a belly still without the least trace of pregnancy.

She made the arrangements quickly, drawing out all the money she had saved to go travelling. It would set back her plans by a year at least – but rather that than have them set back permanently. She rang a clinic, it was the only one she knew of, she had seen an advert in a bus shelter.

154

'Private,' she said, and had an appointment for the next day. It was routine, The doctor wrote down her dates, felt her stomach, asked her when her last period was.

'I'll have a breakdown if I go through with it,' she said desperately. 'I honestly think I'll go mad.'

'That's all right,' the doctor was calm, surprised by her outburst.

'You don't have to convince me – we'll book you in for next week, you're six weeks pregnant now, so next Wednesday, 11 am. Sign this.'

She arranged to stay overnight. It put fifty pounds on the bill, but she knew that she could not walk around the streets.

She had to arrange what to do. She lied to Mac. 'I'm going to stay with Connie in Belfast for a few days.'

He sulked.

'I need a break. She is my closest friend. I want to tell her the news. No, don't see me off at the boat; you know how these things upset me.'

More lies. A note to Connie. 'You must say that I was with you on these dates if anyone ever asks, not that they will, I'm in a fix and need an alibi. My mother thinks I'm visiting you. Much love. Theresa.'

She packed her bag, taking enough for three days, and went out in the morning as though for work, saying she would go straight from there to the ferry. But she caught a taxi to another part of the city.

It was 9.30 when she arrived at the clinic, her knees weak and her palms sweaty. This time the receptionist ushered her into a corridor with doors leading off, and sent her up a flight of stairs. A woman in a white nurses' uniform was waiting for her at the top. She ticked her name off a card and took her to a room.

'Get undressed and into the bed, the medic will be along soon to give you a pre-med.'

Something about Theresa must have made her turn back. She stopped at the door and told her not to look so worried. 'It will all be over by this afternoon,' she said as she left her.

Theresa remembered being moved, she was on a trolley and it went down in a lift. She was pushed along the corridor and through one of the doors. Somebody was screaming, then she lost consciousness.

She was not in pain when she woke, the room was not quite dark and she heard a voice saying, 'I'll just give you something. . .make you sleep. . .make you sleep . . .', and she saw faces peering at her. Her mother with a set of rosary beads was turning round slowly. 'I'm praying for your soul,' she kept saying each time she turned to face her. 'Your soul. . .your soul.'

'This will make you sleep. . . .'

She saw Mac laughing, opening his shirt to show a tattoo on his chest; an enormous red gory heart and he was Jesus because he had a beard, but not a crown of thorns.

'Bless me, Jesus,' her mother prayed, and Mac spread open his palms to receive her.

'Look at Baby Jesus smiling,' Sister Mercy told the class. Theresa was sitting behind a desk. The statue was on a table. She stared at it, but the Virgin held nothing in her arms. The Virgin shook her head, tears fell from her eyes.

'You!' The statue pointed to Theresa. 'You have killed my little baby Jesus!'

'I didn't do it, I didn't do it, Sister!'

'It's all right, there, there. . . . Here's a cup of tea,' a woman said, placing a cup down by her bed. Theresa sat up. The room was sunny.

'Were you having a bad dream? It's just the anaesthetic wearing off.'

Theresa sipped the tea. Why wasn't she in pain?

The doctor came to see her and explained that as it was an early operation they had used suction. Theresa gagged. He went on to say that she might experience some cramping, but that it was all over. He made it sound so easy.

But after the abortion it was not as straightforward. She had not expected to feel so saddened by it, she thought she ought to be relieved. She spent two nights in a bed and breakfast in North Wales when she was supposed to be with Connie. Two days which were foul. She had stopped bleeding and had no pain, but was terrified of feeling any slight twinges. Indigestion made her worry. She was a fugitive hiding in a strange cold room. It rained incessantly. Someone else was crying for her, as dry-eyed she lay awake at night, watching the patterns on the thin curtains which did nothing to stop out the light. For two nights she waited for the dawn, listening to the first sound of birds. Sometimes she paced the room. God knows what the proprietor thought she was doing. He was jolly every morning, talking to the guests while his wife did the rounds with an enormous teapot. They must have thought that she was up to something the questions they asked, trying to work out why a young girl should be staying there alone in the off season.

'Still at school then? Is it half term already?'

'Just having a break from work, is it?'

She must have looked strange. Vague and hardly receptive each morning as she ate her cornflakes ravenously and stared out of the window at the drizzle with unfocused eyes, the dark shadows under them deepening as the day progressed. It was a rule that they should all be out of the place by 10.30. She was always the last to leave her room and the first guest back in the mid-afternoon.

She had no money left. She had cleared out her savings. She just wanted to go back to her home and her job. This time spent hiding was nightmarish. She walked around the town or tried to shelter from the rain, she could not afford to eat. She was hungry but decisive. No one would know, especially Mac: if he ever found out, he would torture her with the knowledge for the rest of her life. He would control her by threatening to tell her parents if she ever stepped out of line or disagreed with him. She would not be owned like that. She felt relief at last when she understood how completely free of him she was, nothing he could say would have any affect on her.

Theresa sat back against the pillows feeling less troubled. She had got Mac out of her life, she had regained her control over events, but even when she reminded herself that she had been younger then and that was the time to make mistakes, she still loathed her stupidity of ten years before.

'Do you want a sleeping pill?' the young nurse asked, wheeling the cocktail cabinet of drugs after her.

Theresa shook her head. She did not want to be full of tranquillizers, pain killers and sleeping pills. Instead she wanted to feel the pain rather than smother it as she had to before. After the abortion there was no time, she could not allow herself the right to mourn. Two days after it she returned home, she went to work, telling those people who asked that yes, she had enjoyed herself at her friend's, and to him she told the total lie, the one which gave her back her life.

'Well, guess what?' she said that first evening back. 'It was all a mistake. I was never pregnant. I got my period while I was over at Connie's. I'm relieved, aren't you?'

Still he kept up the same strange act.

'It would have been nice, wouldn't it!' he said, gazing away into the distance dreamily with a half smile.

But now was the time for truth.

'It would have been hell on earth,' she told him, as all the smiles she had ever acted finally dropped from her face. After that she refused to see him.

'Are you sure you don't want a sleeping pill?' the young nurse persisted. 'You have hardly slept since you've been admitted, have you?'

'Really, I'm OK,' Theresa said, hoping that she would go away. She yawned exaggeratedly.

This time was so different. After a miscarriage, mourning

was approved of. Everyone was on her side, all in it with her, trying to feel her pain and share it among themselves. But what would they have thought if they had known her ten years ago, if somehow they got to hear that she was 'the kind of woman' who had an abortion. And wasn't she lucky because she was able to act swiftly and hide? At least she had been able to spare her parents the knowledge of the fact when they were alive.

'All this messing about with bloody pills, those kind of women won't be able to have babies when they want them. It's not right; it's going against God's plan for the world,' that was what her mother used to say. She believed that it was tit for tat – that was her interpretation of the papal encyclical – control your fertility now and you will frighten it away when you want it. She could still hear her mother's voice. 'Those type of women will end up sterile. If you ask me . . . it would serve them right.'

Theresa had been scared. It was their revenge; once safe into menopause they tortured young women with fears, resenting anyone that had a choice because in their day they had none. Her mother believed in letting them pay for their crimes on earth. Why bother waiting for an after-life?

It could have all been so different. There was a girl in the shoe shop where she had her first job after leaving school. She got to be quite friendly with her. Agnes, that was her name, Agnes Daly. She had not thought about her in years. Her parents were Irish. Funny how you could go through life with lots of different people, but suddenly strike up a rapport with those ones who knew your ways. Agnes only worked there on Saturdays, along with the other college girls. They were all educated, earning pocket money, and they made Theresa feel stupid because she was earning her living. They did her a favour really, because it was the two years she spent there that made her decide to do something different; it was the prospect of being stuck in the shop, putting different shoes on the likes of them to save them bending. But not Agnes, she was different.

They used to have a laugh together, messing about in the stock room trying all the different styles on and mincing up and down the narrow corridor out of earshot of the customers. Agnes was really wild sometimes, but always very proper. She didn't like it when the boss talked smuttily, and she used to stand up to him. She was the one who said to his face that she did not like 'old men to paw at her', that time he tried to get a hold of her in the back room. She announced it clearly so that everyone heard, everyone in the shop, and the area manager on his six-weekly visit. That was not like the others, they crept away into corners to cry, and soft Beryl boasted about it. 'Oh,' she would say giggling and coy, 'Mr Allsway put his hands between my legs when I was up the ladder,' blushing as if it was a compliment.

Theresa started to look forward to Saturdays when Agnes would turn up, and she grew to loathe the weekdays when there was just Beryl, Allsway and Mrs Nicholls. But Agnes left; she came in one Saturday looking frightful and the next week she gave in her notice. She was pregnant and her father had found out and told her to leave home, to go anywhere. All those weeks that Agnes had fretted and worried. She had sworn Theresa to secrecy, told her not to breathe a word to a living soul. Agnes thought that she might know what do do, where to go for help, but Theresa was helpless. She remembered angrily that at the time she had decided if she was ever in the same fix as Agnes she would have committed suicide through shame.

'The disgrace is the worst thing,' the other girl told her, 'when everyone else finds out. My father just wants me to disappear, he can't bring himself to look at me. There's a home for unmarried mothers run by nuns in London, they let you keep the baby if you want. . . .'

A home. Theresa shuddered at the memory. By the time she made her mistake she was three years older and it made all the difference. She had escaped. She wondered what had happened to Agnes after that. Alone in London branded as that kind of girl, and Agnes so young she would have believed it.

Theresa knew that she could face the world, his family and his brothers as a poor young woman of twenty-nine who had miscarried. None of them would want to know her as the poor young woman of nineteen who had terminated her pregnancy. As she thought that, the tears began to pour down her face. She had so much pain, she had been forced to lie for their acceptance, just as she had been forced to terminate the pregnancy for freedom. It was not relief for freedom which overwhelmed her now, but the unresolved mourning rites pushing themselves through like blades, sharp and raw.

After supper the bustle in the ward died down. There was always a lull in the day's activity as the night nurse came on duty. Over on the other side of the ward someone had their light on. The curtains were drawn, the bed and the light absorbed their colour, becoming an orange glow. Theresa's eye took in everything from the top of the clip chart hanging from the bed, the white aluminium frame, the open-weave blankets so that none of the patients would suffocate, to the regulation cupboards, each with their water jug and single glass. She had told a nurse to clear everything out from hers after Auntie Sal left that afternoon. Now it was empty and pristine. Everything was regulated.

Her tired eyes sprang open with a will of their own when she closed them. Her head was starting to throb. She knew that tomorrow she would feel awful. Tomorrow might be time for pain killers, but tonight was for grieving, long overdue. Tonight she would keep watch. Tonight she would grasp at pains as they returned and she would seize them gratefully and hold them in the clear parts of her memory. Tonight she would let herself remember. She understood at last why it had always been a solitary grief, for it could not be shared. It was her act of isolation as well as her gesture of defiance. It was for her alone. Over on the far side, the solitary light went out as the last of the non-sleepers drifted off. She lay in the dark waiting for the first rays of morning, keeping the lonely vigil that she had started ten years before.

The Late Martha Doyle

In the cold parlour, the relatives of the deceased were gathering. They sat on the edge of chairs, stiffly holding their backs away from the antimacassars, and as each new influx of mourners arrived, they huddled together to make room.

Martha Doyle was 'gone'. No one said 'at peace'. That was a euphemism they all avoided, for as she grew older, there was no doubt but she grew wilder, driving her family to despair about all sorts of imaginary events and the visions which she alone saw. She lived the latter part of her life in a parallel existence from which she returned to tell wonderful stories like some medieval traveller and she had bouts of clarity when they would squirm under her direct, green gaze.

Everyone who knew the late Mrs Doyle wanted to pay their last respects: local shopkeepers, neighbours, even the debt collector. But Martha was not laying out. None of her family had the heart to bring her back home after she died quietly in hospital. The irony of that fact was not lost on any of them. She left her turbulent life peacefully; slipping away softly before anyone noticed, and the way they looked at it was that she went out of her house living, and that was how they would remember her. They would not carry her back to be stretched out coldly in this seldom used parlour.

Women twisted black gloves with anxious white hands. Men felt uncomfortable in dark suits. They put their fingers inside shirt collars and rubbed to ease the pressure of starch and stiff linen on the raw skin of their necks.

Laurence Doyle stood over by the door where he could best survey the gathering and be certain of welcoming each new mourner into the room with his firm handshake. He was not sure whether he ought to clasp the proffered hand between both of his, or keep to a more formal gesture. He did not want it said that he singled some out for attention, even if he had forgotten himself entirely when Annie came down. She was that distressed, he had his arm about her thin shoulders before he realized. But then, they always had been close. They banded together, the two youngest and he was, by a couple of years, still her big brother.

He was a well-preserved fellow. He had fixed his black tie in the dressing-table mirror that morning and was satisfied with his reflection. The passing years had not been unkind to him and he was very aware of that as he cast around the room at the rest of his family. When asked, he would give his age as mid-fifties. He was careful to describe it this way ever since he realized how close the next decade had crept. He reminded himself that there was still a good thirteen years between him and the oldest, Jack, who only read of his mother's death in the memorial column and turned up the night before, reeking of drink, and looking a sight in a dusty raincoat and brown trousers. Of all things, thought Laurence, and even then there was a tear in them. One of the sisters stitched him a black armband. It was Stella, good steady Stella who had never married, and even she could not look at his red face as she gave it to him.

'It's that pathetic look of gratitude I can't stand,' she complained to Laurence that morning. 'And anyway, I wasn't doing it for him but for mother.'

All morning they had managed to keep Jack away from the drink, and now he was starting to show signs of impatience.

Laurence felt again along the inside of his collar. He would have liked to loosen his tie. He hated funerals; God knows, he had attended enough. He knew it would not be long before they attended each other's. No matter if he was one of the youngest, he knew that age was no guarantee of death's hierarchy, they would all be called soon enough.

'No one lasts for ever,' the grocer from the corner shop said. But, God knows, his mother had certainly tried. She had hung tenaciously on to life, watching as time stripped her of family, friends, and husbands. It was a terrible life too, a hard, desperate struggle. Yet she would not leave it. It could never have been easy for her. She was only thirty-six when she was widowed for a second time.

'She was that good, to bring up nine of you on her own.' The grocer was going round from one mourner to the next, his accounts book finally scored through for the late Mrs Doyle, outstanding bills cancelled with one stroke of his pen. 'We'll not see the likes of her again. A rare sort.' He shook everyone's hand.

'We appreciate you coming round, Mr Warren. We know you can't easily get away.' Stella spoke to him for a few minutes, before passing him to another of her sisters.

Nine of them, Laurence thought. She had had more, but had not been able to breathe enough life into them, worn out with childbirth. In those days it was a relief that some should not survive. Laurence shuddered. It was different today. He thought fondly about his three daughters, now with children of their own. Yes, he was not in bad shape at all. 'You've never got five grandchildren!' a woman at the bridge club had said only the other week.

As the grocer took his leave, Laurence showed him to the street. He prided himself on saying the correct things, on finding the appropriate words. But today it felt to him as if everyone was searching for something to say, and there was little comfort in politeness. No wonder his mother went in for different ways of doing things. Despite himself he chuckled, and quickly put his hand over his mouth to cover his indiscretion. Mr Warren looked quizzically at him.

'Nerves are strange things,' he whispered before he walked away.

Laurence went inside and resumed his position, looking around restlessly. He hated waiting. That was always the hardest part, standing around until the funeral got under way.

Across the room, a young mother sat nursing a baby. A fair-haired woman with blunt features. That wasn't his niece surely? Time passed so quickly, he had not seen her for more than a year, not since that last Christmas when they all got together because one of the boys was home from America. And she was not expecting then, he was sure of it.

The baby clapped its hands together. He watched its strong arms reaching out as it was lifted up by a cooing relative. Passed around from one lap to another all morning, it was surprisingly good-natured. Laurence's wife was tickling the child and laughing. She turned and, noticing her husband, waved the baby's hand at him. He waved back, feeling years drop away. Once, she looked just like that with a baby on her knee, in a room crowded as this for another funeral.

His Uncle Alec suffered a massive heart attack one night after work. It took them all by surprise. Nervously, Laurence put his hand to his chest, remembering how Alec never had a day's illness in his life. At the time everyone blamed Alec's wife. They said that if Betty had looked after him properly he might still be alive. It was all the overtime he put in. He had killed himself to provide her with enough money for fancy holidays and smart clothes. At the funeral they were all embarrassed by her grief. She was in a state of collapse and had to be helped from the church into one of the hired cars.

They had all expected their mother to be in a worse

state. Their anxieties and nerves were shredded on her account, not for the widow.

'What will we do if mother has one of her funny turns?' Annie asked. 'Alec was always her favourite brother. I suppose it was because he was so much younger than her. You'd think he was her son, the way she carried on about him.'

'He was good to her. That's why. Don't ever forget, Annie Doyle, that you were allowed to stay on at school because he paid mother regular money to keep this house together, while the rest of us had to go out and work.' Stella's look was hard.

'And you, Laurie Doyle,' she said, wagging her finger at him. 'You two got the education none of us had, thanks to Uncle Alec.'

He remembered how Jack sneered. 'Well, will all their fancy education help us to deal with mam? That's what I'd like to know.'

But Stella turned her back to him and continued to talk to the others.

Between them they planned delaying tactics. They worked out how to stagger their mother's arrival so that she would be the last in and the first out.

'The least time she spends there the easier it will be for us all.'

'Annie had even tried to suggest that she stay at home and welcome the mourners back from the cemetery, but when they put that idea to her, she would have none of it.

'What? And miss the burial!'

Martha Doyle was insistent; her jaw set, her mouth a straight, if twitching, line of determination. They had seen that look before; the bloodless mark of her compressed lips, drawn like a dotted line across her face, hinting at something yet to come.

'We can't stop her. She'll get to Alec's funeral even if we tell her a different day.'

The family rolled their eyes, muttered, prayed and

reminded each other of the urgent need to keep an eye on her.

'Don't leave me on my own with her,' one of the Doyle sisters pleaded, rubbing her pregnant belly. 'I won't be able to lift her and if she falls on me I'm done for.'

'It's all right,' Stella said, 'I'll keep as close by her as I can, and someone will have to walk behind her at all times. Arnold, Vincent, keep close by her. Our Laurence can make sure that she is not left alone with the coffin. The shock of seeing it might be too much.'

Annie was terrified and Laurence remembered how his wife, usually a calm, unflappable woman, became nervous after all the planning that was necessary.

'You never know what she's going to do,' she whispered to him.

'Don't worry,' he reassured her. 'You'll see, my mam will behave perfectly.'

On the day of the funeral everything progressed well. Martha was regal in a mauve hat with a veil. She was having a day out and waved one hand to passers-by from the chief mourner's car.

Alec's widow, having taken a sedative, sat cramped between two of the Doyle sisters, who passed her clean hankies in a never-ending supply. In the front Martha was placed next to one of their uncles. If the vein on his temple bulged slightly he gave no other outward sign of anxiety.

'I think me mother's going to be OK,' one of the girls whispered to Laurence, biting her nails.

All Martha Doyle's brood kept silent watch on her. From the car to the plot, they walked alongside, behind, and in front of her. The mother, unsuspectingly flanked by the children.

'Lovely day,' she said conversationally to them, flattered by all the attention.

The coffin was carried by Alec's two brothers, and four trade union officials. Six strong men in dark suits. The family stood tensely as they waited for the coffin's descent into earth. The priest began the prayers over the grave, Alec's wife swooned and was caught in time by one of her nephews.

There were nearly fifty people around that grave; the extended family, work mates, and the neighbours who followed on behind the procession. People pushed forward as the grave diggers passed earth around on the end of their shovels, and the mourners threw soil on top of the coffin.

'Ashes to ashes, dust to dust.'

The workmen, sweating and covered in mud, moved among the soberly dressed mourners. They had worked double rate that morning. There was a burial alongside this one, so they had opened up two lots without time for a break. They would probably not have time to get this one covered before the next group arrived, and the priest went through the same routine at the next grave. Laurence thought that the priest was cutting it fine, but it would give the grave diggers something to talk about in the pub later; how they were rushing them in like tourists, one hearse no sooner left than another screeched to a halt.

Laurence remembered that it was Annie who suddenly dug him in the ribs.

'Holy God!' she said, 'I can't see my mother.'

He looked over his shoulder, still with his handful of earth ready, but as they were at the front he could not see what was happening.

'She'll be at the back with Stella,' he said, throwing the last scattering of soil before the grave diggers started to pile spadeful after spadeful.

It was only then that he noticed how quite a few mourners were facing the wrong way, backs toward the grave. He heard muttering, a woman's voice saying, 'One minute she was here, the next, I looked around . . .'

'Well, I thought she was at the front with our Laurence . . . I didn't know where she was, did I?'

That was Stella's unmistakable voice, high with indignation. He felt his stomach churn. Mother! he thought. They heard shouting.

'Martha! Martha! Jesus, Mary and Joseph! Somebody help me get her out.'

'Stand back, give her air. Leave her room to breathe.'

They pushed their way through and saw their uncle in his shirt sleeves.

'Help me pull her up!' he shouted.

The men took off jackets and began rolling up their cuffs.

'Oh, isn't it awful?' one of his sisters said.

'She must have stepped backwards. I never noticed. I thought she was down at the front with you. Then I heard praying coming from that open grave and I looked down and saw . . .' but her voice tailed away, unable to speak the awful name. At length she whispered weakly

'. . . our mother.'

'We'll get her out,' someone said bravely.

It took the combined efforts of all the pall bearers to heave Martha up. She lay where they rolled her at the grave's mouth. Muddy and saturated, she stared up at the sky and began to sing. 'Out of the depths I have called to you, Oh Lord . . .'

The priest finished the prayers for the dead over Alec's grave, trying not to hurry, while aware of the possibility of being called to administer Extreme Unction. But Martha was coming round. She laughed; every eye was on her. She put her hand up to fix her hair.

'It's natural, you know,' she told the spectators, for there was quite a crowd gathered as the other funeral party had arrived, anxious to claim their grave.

'Now, look here!' said the man from Brennan and Sons, Funeral Directors, 'We arranged this burial to take place at a quarter past. You had plenty of notice, we put it in the *Echo*.'

The official from MacCormack's Chapel of Rest shrugged. 'It's one of those unforeseeable events. I am sorry. I will try to move my client's party as soon as possible, but you must understand that sometimes grief makes people behave in ways . . .'

'Don't talk to me about grief,' Brennan's man interrupted. 'I know everything there is to know about grief. I've been in this business for twenty-nine years.'

He stepped back and tilted his head so that he could scrutinize the younger man. 'This just isn't good enough!' He turned away and holding both hands up, waved for the pall bearers to stop. 'Put the casket back in the hearse,' he shouted over people's heads.

The coffin stopped ten paces away from the car while the pall bearers wondered whether they could turn round without letting it drop.

'Back into the hearse,' their boss repeated, gesticulating wildly.

'How are we going to do that?' a bearer on the right side whispered, being careful not to turn his head.

'We'll have to count our paces,' said the man behind.

'All right then? Now, all together with your left feet, after two.'

Staring straight ahead, the men walked solemnly backwards, counting one two, one two, with each pace.

The man from Brennan's attempted to get his party back to the cars. He was very professional, he apologized for the delay and assured them that they would only have a slight wait. But one of the chief mourners wanted to know more.

'What do you mean?' He stared at MacCormack's man, stupefied. 'What are you telling me, that the grave's occupied?'

'No, no, you don't understand,' he told him. 'She's out, she's just coming round. . . .'

'Jesus Christ!' The enquirer raced back to his party.

All around there was confusion, and in some parts, panic.

'How could anybody make a mistake like that?' someone

was saying. 'I mean, I know some people are slow, but you think they'd catch on.'

'I don't understand how this could have happened. How could anyone sleep through all that banging?'

'What banging?'

'You know, when they nail the top down.'

'You mean this one wasn't dead?' said a passing woman who had come to lay flowers.

The man from Brennan's ushered those remaining from his party back towards the cars, from where the chanting of the rosary soon became audible.

Stella, her arms held tight across her chest to control her anger, watched from a distance.

'Ah, she's made up, getting all the attention. That's what she's after. You'll see; she'll be as right as rain in half an hour. Don't upset yourself Annie, she's not dying yet. She'll outlast the lot of us, that one.'

Annie cried into her handkerchief and knelt beside her mother.

'Oh, I felt myself going,' Martha told her. 'And then I thought, I'm getting on a bit, I might as well stay here. You never know when you are going to be called.'

She blessed herself, leaving muddy marks across her chest at the four points of the compass.

'If we'd known you were just getting some practice in we'd have left you down there,' one of the brothers said, wiping mud from his sleeve. 'Look at this suit, it's got to go back tomorrow.'

The trouser bottoms were covered in brown clay. The men were sweating, their shoes sodden.

'We look like we've come off a building site. Some funeral this turned out to be.'

The priest came towards them holding the container of holy water ready to administer the last rites.

'She's all right, Father, she doesn't need it, she's coming round.'

But Annie was not so sure. She had knelt, listening to

her mother throughout, and she noticed how Martha was talking about herself in the past tense. Martha had decided that it must be her funeral. When she saw the priest, her suspicions were confirmed. She started to make a last confession.

Stella hung back. Irritation lined her face. 'She knows what she's up to . . . any minute now it will be "Father, I've had fourteen children". . . you wait for it.'

Laurence laughed, remembering how accurate Stella was. As the priest drew close, Martha sat up and began to tell the priest her life story.

'Father, I've had nine children . . . well, I had more, you know. . . . I had twelve, but the Good Lord called some home. Bless me, Father. I've had thirteen children . . . no, I haven't, have I?'

'No, you're right,' Stella suddenly shouted, unable to conceal her rage.

Her mother continued softly, ignoring the interruption.

'Bless me, Father, but I've had fourteen children,' she smiled, 'and my hair's still curly. It's white, but it's natural,' she laughed. 'These curls are my own, it's not a perm you know, Father. After fourteen children it's still curly.'

'Oh, the liar!' Stella said. 'I put a Tweenie-twink in it for her two weeks ago. I can't stand it. I can't listen to her any more. It's always the same, gangs of imaginary children and naturally curly hair.'

'Oh, Stella,' Annie sobbed, 'what can we do?'

'There's not much, is there?' Stella snapped. Then with a wave of her hand she dismissed her. 'Let her make her last confession,' she said, resigned to the event.

'Bless me, Father, but I'm sixty-nine.'

'Sixty-three! You're sixty-three!' Stella shouted, not wanting to hear any further nonsense. 'Father, this woman, Martha Doyle, is sixty-three and she had nine children. I am one of them and can vouch for the truth and accuracy of this information.' She turned towards her mother.

'And you are sixty-three,' she told her coldly. Then talking hold of her arm she began to pull her from the graveside. Martha stared uncomprehendingly. She looked around, then finally recognized Stella. Whispering, she asked her what she was doing and rolled her eyes theatrically.

'I've passed over,' she told her daughter. 'I must have. It wasn't half a funny feeling. Is that all there is to it? Should I hold my hands like this?' she asked, crossing them over her chest. 'Or is it better like this?'

'Oh, do get up for God's sake, mother!' Stella snapped.

The late Martha Doyle let herself be hoisted up from the grass obediently.

'Why are all the family here?' she whispered.

'Why do you think?' Stella muttered cynically.' We're having a party.'

She led her towards the black hired cars that stood in a row.

'Get in the car,' she instructed, her voice cracking under the strain. 'And put your hat straight!'

'Am I going to meet Him?'

Stella did not answer, but pushed her mother in front of her. As the shiny black vehicle sped out of the cemetery, Martha went rigid.

'Oh God, not another funny turn,' Stella moaned, burying her face in her hands as her mother remained erect like a soldier on parade. Later they understood that it was the large wrought-iron gates leading to the avenue which caused her sudden formality. As they passed through them Martha had been convinced that she was about to be judged and she wanted to make a good impression.

As the remainder of the cortege followed on, one of the brothers looked around. 'Where's Betty?' he asked.

In the commotion, Alec's widow had been forgotten about entirely. Laurence and some others ran back. They found her in a sedated haze staring at the wreaths on her husband's grave.

'I don't want to be any trouble,' she said, as they helped her into the car, which had to reverse the length of the drive. For the first time Laurence felt his heart go out to Alec's wife.

Now he looked over to where Betty sat in the parlour. That was quite a blue rinse she'd put in her hair, he thought. She never remarried and lived alone in eternal mourning. She sat in the room without touching any of her in-laws, keeping the distance between them physical. Laurence admired Betty; she must have been seventy, although no one knew her exact age, she was slightly older than Alec when they married; and here she was, still sprightly, always neatly turned out.

A few years after Alec's death, the family had altered their collective opinion about her. It was as if someone passed the word around and on cue they all picked up the idea that deep down Betty was not a bad sort, just a bit frosty on the surface. But the chill never quite left, it hung around, making them reluctant to squash up against her on the sofa and make space in the parlour.

A trickle of black motors began to pull up outside the house. There was a fluttering of spirits as the realization that the funeral was about to start settled in everyone's mind. Eyes flickered, looked up and swiftly away again. Laurence felt relieved; the waiting was over. Arnold, who was acting as the oldest son in place of Jack, pulled out a list and began to marshal people into groups for their positions in the cars.

'Vincent and Pauline, Thadeus and Mary, Laurence and Brid, can you go into the first car? Stella, will you go with Annie and Bill, oh . . . Thadeus and Vincent can you take Jack with you?'

The list went on while outside, more or less sober with just the trace of a shake, Jack was helped into a car. Laurence sat back next to him. He looked back to see where Stella was. She always reckoned that their mother did everything for attention. She said that Martha was only happy when she was at the centre of everything. If that was so, he thought, she would be happy today at the centre of her own spectacle. But it didn't seem right, this sober procession of mourners after such an outlandish life. If the late Martha Doyle had been able to do anything about it, he knew that she would have insisted on having a bit of a hooley, rather than this strange last rite. Overwhelmed by sadness he sank further into the seat. He looked out of the back window and saw Stella waiting with Annie and her husband. Annie was clutching a hankie, and he could not be sure, but it looked as if Stella too was crying, or had come as near to it as she ever would.

The church was packed for the funeral service, because it was Martha's parish, and many of the congregation turned out. As the immediate family walked down the aisles to the benches reserved for them at the front, Stella thought wryly that this was as close as she would ever get to being a bride as she endured the slow walk as the organ played. To think that her mother did that twice, and buried both her husbands, changing the festive white dress (which she let out to accommodate her second wedding) for widow's weeds.

They took mourning very seriously then. She remembered as a child when her father died, they all had to wear black. She could not have been more than ten, even Laurence and Annie, who was no more than a baby, were dressed in dark colours. And for months after they had to wear it, changing the shade to purple, then to lavender. Martha was exhausted dyeing all their things out in the big tin bath in the back kitchen. The steam was terrible, her mother burst all the veins in her face. It seemed then as if she spent her life washing, pounding clothes in the dolly tub, always hanging things up in the yard where there was no sun. Oh God, no, she thought, she did not regret being unmarried.

Occasionally she had twinges when she saw Annie, whose unexpected late marriage produced the niece she was so fond of. Exactly like Annie when she was younger, Fiona was dark-eyed and soft-hearted. And a lot more bloody sensible, she reminded herself sharply, than her sister had ever been.

Stella watched her niece come into the church. She loved that girl, there was no doubt about it. She felt almost as if she were her own. She had been with Annie all the time she was pregnant, and had held the tiny baby just a few minutes after she was born. What more did she need?

All morning she had been extraordinarily tense. As she arrived at the church, she felt as if a spring had unwound and she had to sit on the pew, unable to kneel. She stared at the altar so that no one would try and speak to her; she concentrated on the flames of the candles which burned into points of light. The red lamp was a blood stain high on the wall. And under it was her own flesh and blood, lying coldly. But her mother had a good innings on earth. It was her, Stella, who was anaemic. She was the one who lost blood all the time, never her mother. Strong-as-a-horse-Martha, while she was the one who needed to take iron supplements all her adult life. She used to feel so tired. Her mother was like a maniac with too much energy; she'd enough for both of them, that one. That's the price you pay. Go through life like Martha it's not surprising something inside goes wrong. The woman's nerves must have worn right through.

Stella imagined nerves like the strings in a piano. They snapped, leaving an empty soundless gap. But it was she who felt empty; her mother was dead. She fixed her eyes on the blood-lit lamp, but it was not blood, it was wax. Her mother was like that now, waxy and cold. Her mother was gone, and she felt for the first time the sheer terror of loneliness.

The church was hot. The candles seemed to burn her and she was glad to get outside after the service and feel the wind on her face for a few moments before joining the cars which would take them to the cemetery.

Just as the procession went through the gates, Annie caught Stella's eye. It was as if she told her a joke, because Stella started to laugh, and could not stop. She was remembering how the late Martha Doyle behaved at Alec's funeral. Annie, caught up with tension, began to laugh too.

At the graveside, Laurence felt a sudden, inexplicable urge to guffaw as he stood looking down into the freshly dug earth. Their mother's spirit had caught them all as if she was there, just out of view, dancing some mad reel to music of her own making. Martha was urging them to have a drink on her; go on, enjoy yourselves!

A ripple of laughter passed from one mourner to another, an undercurrent which made them twitch. They put their hands to their mouths as they each remembered something that Martha had said, something she had done. It was as if she was whispering in their ears.

The priest intoned, 'Out of the depths I have called to Thee, Oh Lord. Lord hear my voice.'

Suddenly a full-throated laugh escaped from towards the back, indecently cutting the prayer in half. It was followed by a terrible silence. The priest glanced up and then away. 'Let thine ears be attentive to the voice of my supplication.'

Another unchecked laugh sounded from the middle of the group, as the crude mirth pushed its way to the front to stand at the grave's edge, unashamed and cackling. The priest breathed out slowly, but did not lift his eyes from the book. He held his finger firmly on the printed line, stopping for no more than a second. 'If thou, O Lord, wilt observe iniquities, Lord, who shall endure them?'

This time the laugh was communal as more and more mourners were caught in its power. The sound of it echoed, multi-voiced. The mourners struggled for control, but misery became hysteria and teased the absurd sound from them. The bereaved were mentally clutching their sides and all the way back to Martha's house, the black limousines stung with the occasional sound of unsuppressible laughter.

Two weeks after the funeral the relatives met again to sort out Martha's things. She did not leave too many possessions. For someone who spent a lot of time imagining reality, it seemed correct that she should leave few material effects. There were a few boxes with letters and photographs in them, but no one understood why they had been important to her, or even if they had. She could have put them in boxes simply to keep the house tidy. There were lots of empty paper bags and broken hair-grips, elastic bands and single lost buttons that would have been stitched back on in time. There were dozens of postcards, most of which they had sent her over the years, although there was a single card from Stockholm, years old because it was addressed to her maiden name, although none of them could make out the date on the postmark. It had the single word 'greetings' on the back. There were brown faded photographs of people none of them knew, a group of sailors, children in wide-brimmed hats and crocheted dresses that swept all the way down to their ankles.

'God knows who these are,' Stella said, 'but I remember those dresses. Me mam made me one of those for the May procession. We all had them.'

There were tall men in tweed caps, and austere looking women, but there were no names on any of the photos.

'We'll never know,' Annie remarked, looking at a picture of a small girl on a sea-shore nursing a cat.

'Well, you wouldn't expect her to label things, now would you?' her husband said, shifting boxes. 'She was as mad as a hatter that one. God, you never knew what she was going to do next.'

Laurence came up into the loft behind him and started laughing, remembering how Martha one night took a turn under the clothes pulley. She lay staring up at the washing, talking about the gleaming white of angels' wings. Annie was horrified because her mother was behaving like a sleepwalker and she had heard that they ought not to be disturbed. She thought that the shock of being woken would kill her and she knelt in tears on the floor, with her mother's head between her hands, while Laurence paced up and down the hall. He said the shock of coming round in the kitchen would kill her, more likely, because she was expecting to be surrounded by angels, not piles of under-clothes. They laughed at the recollection, even Annie.

'And she sat up after, and said what a fool she was. She always got that in, she used to tell you always, because you were the serious one,' she said to Stella. But she was not amused.

'She always played on it,' she told them. 'She used to act soft if she was in the wrong.'

Stella knew that her mother exploited her eccentricity during tense situations. Like the time the rent money went missing. When Martha went rigid and began singing hymns, Stella knew she must have spent it.

They laughed until Stella reminded them acidly that she always behaved the same way. Martha would lie on the floor recovering her senses, with an audience of onlookers, telling absolute strangers that she had innumerable children.

'You might laugh now,' she said, 'but I mind that day in Davis's when she went down behind the bread counter. Saturday morning it was and the shop was packed with people, they were queuing up in the street getting loaves for the weekend, and the next thing I knew she was on the lino telling the baker's wife her life history and about the gangs of imaginary kids.

'And that time I went to see her in hospital, the first thing the nurse said to me as I went in was what an extraordinary woman my mother was, she said she had no idea that I came from such a big family. God, it was big enough without her exaggerating. What did she thing she was achieving? Sympathy?

'And then, she'd recover and sit up. Look all around the room and say, "Wasn't I a bloody fool, Stella?"'

'Aye,' Laurence said, looking at Stella, 'we'll all miss her, too.'

Stella's eyes grew bright and she looked away. No one had accused her of loving her mother too much. She was the hardened sister. She struggled for control; busying herself with packing cases, pulling things out and putting them back in, in a meaningless ritual. No one was fooled. Annie began to cry into a handkerchief, and even her husand had to wipe his nose.

Stella stood up abruptly, her face pale and tired, suddenly old. She went downstairs silently.

'She's really unset, poor Stella. She's the one who is going to be here all on her own. She'll miss Mam, more than any of us.'

Annie sobbed without restraint.

Downstairs Stella took her coat from the peg and went out. They thought she had taken herself for a walk. What they failed to notice was the envelope she pushed into her pocket. She opened the door. Upstairs, they heard it close softly.

At the end of the street, Stella waited for a bus. It took her out to an area of the city she was not familiar with. She had to ask strangers for directions and a woman looked at her and said, 'Not from round here then, love?' Stella felt insecure as she shook her head. She had not come out this way for years and everything had changed. The streets were wider here, and there were trees in them. It took her half an hour to find the correct street. She knocked on the door, and was relieved when Betty opened it, a familiar face at last. She ushered Stella in.

'Excuse my slippers,' she said, looking puzzled, 'only I wasn't expecting anyone.'

Stella stood by the fireplace. She was vague and reluctant

to talk. Betty knew that it was not a social visit. Something had shocked her. She watched as Stella nervously fingered a buff envelope. She said nothing. Betty glanced at it and looked away. Stella was struggling with her memory, trying to recall details of something that happened when she was very young, so young that it passed into the grey area of dreams and half-imagined ideas.

'I had to talk to someone,' she said lamely.

Betty nodded as Stella talked intermittently, leaving sentences unfinished. It was only when she mentioned a photograph that Betty became alert and started to ask questions.

'Tell me what you remember,' she said with unusual authority.

'There used to be a photograph that hung over the fireplace in my grandmother's house. Two babies both the same age or so. One was my uncle Alec. I remember gran saying wasn't he nice when he was a baby. It was one of those tinted photos and you could see the pencil lines where the eyelashes had been drawn in. I used to think that I'd be nice if someone took a big picture of me and painted in rosy cheeks and bits of curls. I hated that photo.

'And the other baby; I think he was called Colm. Gran said that he had been my uncle's little friend. He died when just a baby. Funny, because I always knew that Colm wasn't my uncle, yet I still thought that he was my gran's. The photograph was taken down after gran died. I don't know what happened to it.'

'It's here,' Betty said.

Stella looked shocked.

'After his mother died, Alec took the photo. It hung in the parlour for a while over the piano, but Alec was never fond of it. I think it embarrassed him. It's in the attic, I can bring it down, if you'd like.'

She sprang up, despite her years, eager to do something, but Stella shook her head and looked curiously at her.

'The other baby?' she asked.

'Alec's little friend?' Betty stopped in the doorway and looked squarely at Stella. 'You know, I used to wonder how Alec could be so stupid. Your father knew, God rest him,' she blessed herself. 'You see, she could only have been sixteen when she had the baby.'

Slowly Stella took the certificate out from the envelope. The older woman came back into the room and took it from her. When she came to the line, 'Father unknown', she almost spat.

'He bloody wasn't! The father was a Swede, a merchant seaman she met down at the docks. Your grandmother told me. I asked her about the photo. Only because one of the babies was my husband. That's how I found out. She told me how he used to send your mother postcards. She was a young girl, she had them round her dressing-table mirror. He was away at sea and the baby died before he returned. He never saw his son. I suppose it's sad, but who knows? It's hard to tell without knowing anything about him.'

'But what happened then?'

'They went away together, to Hull, I think. She was married to him by now . . . God help her! He abandoned her, the swine! She came back three years later, saying that he had run out on her. The awful thing was that she was pregnant again, and wouldn't you know . . . the police turned up looking for her. Seems he was already married in Sweden and their marriage was invalid. He had gone to sea again by this time.'

'So then she had that second baby adopted,' Stella chipped in, beginning to see the story unfold.

'Indeed not. She took up with Liam Shawcross very quickly, she was married in a hurry to her first husband. He's not Jack's father. Well, he was in name, and down on the certificate. To be honest, I don't think he knew. And then she had Vincent and Thadeus very quickly one after the other. Now they are proper Shawcrosses. Then Liam died and Martha married your father, and went on and had six more. Well, she had another to Shawcross, which didn't live beyond the first year, and I know that she lost two to your father. You see she really did have thirteen. All those times she used to say she had more than a dozen, do you remember? And you used to tell her to behave herself!' Betty was laughing now. 'I know her mind was wandering but she wasn't that far from the mark after all!'

'How do you know that the seaman was Jack's father?' Stella asked, her voice subdued.

Something about her look made Betty stop.

'Martha told me. She walked all the way out here one evening, on her own, and stood at that door. I brought her in and made her some tea and I remember thinking that if she was going to have a turn, I'd never be able to cope on my own. But she was as lucid as I've ever seen her. She told me she just wanted someone to know. She was disturbed though, I think she wanted to tell me about Colm you see, but couldn't bring herself to speak the name. So I just left it. She never knew that any of us had been told about it.'

She shook her head slowly, and smiled.

'Thirteen children!' she said, raising her eyebrows.

'Fourteen,' Stella said, her face white. She pulled out a letter.

'Does this date mean anything to you?'

Betty took the scrap of paper from her and scrutinized it carefully.

'That's before Jack was born. That must have been during the time she was with that foreigner. Good God . . . she not only came back without a husband, but without her baby. What does it say?'

She squinted her eyes up at the neat copperplate, but without her reading glasses she could not attempt it. Stella sat down heavily. She was breathing hard. It was a note from a witness. The late Martha Doyle, then called something else, had signed away her rights as a mother, and left her baby, never to see it again. She was nineteen years old.

'I didn't know anything about this. I doubt if even your dad did.'

Neither women spoke much. The clock ticked. Betty cleared her throat.

'I don't think you should tell the others,' she said at last. 'That must have been what she wanted to tell me that day, but even then she couldn't speak about it. It would do them no good to hear this.'

But Stella understood how her mother had told them, told them constantly. 'We just never listened, that's all.'

Later that evening when Stella returned home she found Annie and her daughter waiting to make sure she was all right.

'Put the kettle on, Fiona,' she shouted as she came in. 'There's a girl. I just want to put some things out of the way.'

She went purposefully upstairs and locked the envelope back safely in the metal box in which Martha Doyle once kept all her papers. She locked it and put the key inside the wardrobe. It was hers now.

Fiona carried a cup of tea to her and asked her if she was going to stay in the bedroom all evening. 'It's freezing here.'

But Stella was thinking about death. 'If anything happens to me,' she said, 'I want you to know where the key to this box is. There's important documents and stuff in here: all medical cards for one thing, and the life assurance premiums. I'm showing you, just in case anything happens. You are the one I'll leave it all to. Do you understand, Fiona? You will have to explain everything to Annie, or decide not to.'

'Explain what?' Fiona laughed.

But Stella was silent. She wanted the girl to possess the secret after her death. She could trust it to Fiona. She watched her trying to keep warm. She probably thought that it was strange how a funeral could bring out the morbidity in people. The young were convinced of their immortality. Stella knew that her niece resolved to live forever. She sent her downstairs and sat alone in the unheated room without moving. She did not notice how cold it had become. She was thinking about her mother, once young, once immortal, as she had never seen her. If she closed her eyes she saw her mother's face as she had known her, old and lined, the late Martha Doyle who returned from the dead, lying by the open muddy grave.

No, the late Martha Doyle would not vanish just like that. Stella knew that she would still be around. And she would be the first to recognize her. In a crowd, Stella knew that she would be able to pick out her mother's distinctive style of walking, the slow shuffling steps and the meandering route she always took. She would follow her as she walked backwards, forwards, or dart sideways to avoid collision with someone only she could see. If she became oblivious to the rest of the world, it was her way of escaping because she had suffered too much while in it.

She would talk to the dead as readily as to the living, and finally she left them to join a companion no one else could see.

And she had spent so much of her life shouting into the deaf ears of her family, wanting to tell them the truth. Stella wondered if she had managed to give them the run around in hospital just once before her death. She knew that Martha would have preferred to go raving, but maybe she saw that there was nothing more to shout over, maybe she told the nurses how many children she had given birth to and without contradiction, was content.

That was Stella's wish for her. She hoped that when there was no one to correct her, Martha had told someone. After all she had been trying to tell her all her life.

'I've had fourteen children. . .wasn't I a bloody fool, Stella?'

'. . . and of the Un-holy Ghost'

Thinking back; when I first met Celeste it must have been around the time that her divorce was going through. Celeste is not her real name. Her real name is something much earthier but it does not describe her. It came from a great-aunt, whose feet were firmly planted in solid Mayo mud, and for whom divorce would have been unthinkable. There is nothing transient or shifting about Celeste's origin. Even the saints she prayed to as a girl were heavy and stoical, earthbound and made flesh. The name started as a joke. I do not know who first called her Celeste, but being so accurate it stuck, for Celeste was ethereal. People would look twice, as if their eyes played tricks.

I was surprised to learn that she was getting a divorce. I had not expected her to be married; she seemed untouched by events, not ready for birth, marriage, and death.

She did not allow the passage of time to intensify the experience. She never held a magnifying glass to the tiniest detail of her life, or hunted for signs which pointed the way to divorce, or even saw herself as the innocent party.

Celeste did not need to look for signs: the divorce was in the air even on the wedding day, but she went ahead with it regardless. And then there had been Chloe.

I suppose the final custody order was made about the

time that she moved into the spare room in N's house. That was how I got to know her. I used to drop by at N's and she would be there. I would see the edge of her back, leaning against the door jamb in the other room, and just the side of her arm protruding from the doorway, as with her back towards us, she silently boiled a kettle. On crossing the landing I might see the soles of her shoes turned up towards me, before the bathroom door closed, and later I would know that the damp soap, the thumb-mark in the toothpaste tube, the hastily folded towel, were the impressions of Celeste.

Each time I called round, I was aware of her growing presence. Where once she used to be in the corner of the room, or softly waiting by a half-open door with its promise of escape, she would be found gradually moving to the centre, stopping to rest lightly in an armchair, maybe reading a book, not ready yet to be drawn into conversation. It was not that she became louder, more obvious or placed herself in front of me. She did none of these things, yet she drew me towards her as if there was no one else in the room, and all around us nothing, empty space and only Celeste. Yet it was with shock I realized how I had stopped going round to see N. I used him solely as a pretext. When he phoned, I would imagine her in the room with him, I would hear her breathing and would strain for the sound of her movements behind his voice.

Everything I learned about Celeste, in those early days, came from him. It was N who told me that she had a child, N who told me about the divorce; and when it came through, N told me the decree had been delivered. When Celeste talked she did not mention the past. Sometimes I thought that we, N and I, had imagined her past because it was revealed to us so sparsely, until we became the authors of some sad fiction, embellishing it until the starting point, Celeste, was no longer present and had faded out of her own story.

Celeste turned herself into a ghost, a shadow that could

vanish as she talked. She was never completely in a room, never totally with anyone, because part of her was always elsewhere, searching for Chloe. Celeste could only keep watch from a distance, she could only protect with her desire, her invisible hands. All her information was culled from different sources; from an ex-neighbour, from a shop assistant where she used to shop, even from the garage mechanic.

Once, when she was desperate, she wrote to her mother-in-law's house. She typed the address on the machine in work so that they would not see her handwriting. If, on his rare monthly visit, her ex-husband happened to see and recognize her hand, he would rip the letter to fragments before his mother had a chance to read it. He would allay the evil one's influence, the woman whose power he might feel, pouring out through the characters in the envelope. But Celeste made one miscalculation; she forgot that in a semi-literate house, what would come through the door apart from circulars and bills? Her letter landed on the mat like a shout, and three months passed before Celeste heard anything. What would the old woman do? Had she managed to hide it, or had she been discovered? Celeste did not know if further contact would become impossible because of her rash action.

A reply did come. She was shocked to see the shaky, unformed letters, spelling out a nervous message. It begged her not to write again and gave a time when she could telephone. The old woman's writing was unlooped, the letters not joined up. There were capitals everywhere, standing out in the middle of words like warnings, stressing the need to be furtive. The scrap of paper, torn from a wrapper, dreaded detection. Celeste saw how the woman had laboured to write it, and was grateful.

When I had been aware of Celeste's presence for nearly a year (I can't say that in that time I knew her) we were sitting around at N's one evening, just a few friends drinking wine and talking. Celeste had been in and out of the room all night, unable to settle. She was agitated with a fervency I did not associate with her. She was like a wild creature, something small and timid. Something quick that disappears, avoiding capture by its ability to hide at the first hint of danger, yet can still be fierce over its young. I remember how white her knuckles were, as she took the cigarette which someone offered her. After two attempts she lit it, but forgot what she was holding. Only when it had burned down to a stub did she remember it, guiding it to her mouth experimentally, like a schoolchild who has stolen one from some adult's pocket.

When she talks, her head moves with the pecking nod of shy people being introduced for the first time, when they dip their heads from nervousness. With Celeste everything is the first time. She leaves gaps between words, frightened that if she puts them too close together there will be no way out.

'All I want is to be kept informed. I have the right to that surely?'

I heard her voice talking to N. She did not sound sure, she did not sound like someone who knew she had a right to anything.

I moved towards them and admit now, with embarrassment, that I used the pretence of filling up their glasses. She looked up sharply, catching my eyes with such a questioning look, that I felt I ought to supply answers where for so long there had been nothing but silences.

'Well, what do you think?' she demanded almost rudely.

Celeste had decided not to waste time with civility. I did not know what to think, not because I do not have opinions, but to form them I find it helpful to have some facts before me. I told her this, as she held her empty glass out. As I poured red wine, she watched me. I felt under scrutiny and made to go away, but she put out her free hand and caught my arm.

'I do need to talk to someone. I need another opinion.'

That was how we became friends. Friendships are founded on the oddest things. Ours was founded on her need for an opinion and my curiosity.

That night she talked freely and fast, words tripping over themselves in their hurry to be heard. I remember her banging the table with her fist, angrily.

'They don't understand that when I lost custody, something in me died. I gave up. I knew what I was doing as I gave her up to them. But why do they want to make it even harder, by denying me the right to know what my daughter is doing? I have no say in her life.

'I have no power to turn her against them, and I wouldn't want to. All I want is to be kept informed. I must have the right to that surely? They have done everything they can to prevent me from seeing her. What do they think? That I would try to take her back now, after all this time, when she doesn't know who I am? Why would any mother take their child away from its only security? His family were right to step in when they did. You see, I couldn't cope.

'I was living in one room, with her father, and we kept arguing. There was nowhere to go where we did not have to listen to the sound of the baby crying, and that wore me down. I couldn't sleep, I was so tense, and then she would start to cry again. I suppose we were both bad-tempered, light-headed through sleeplessness. I would walk around, pushing the pram, disorientated as a sleepwalker. I felt as though I was dead. I used to watch other mothers in the park, happy with their babies and wonder what was wrong with me. He said I was unnatural.

'We had no money. I had to leave my job, he wasn't working but he would not stay in to look after her. We were both so young then, and now we have both changed. He must have. It's funny, but whenever I think of him, I think of this unemployed boy – I don't think of him the way he must be now. I've heard that he's quite successful; with a front to keep up at work. I don't think that anybody there knows that he has a child. Well, he doesn't have to look after her, does he? His mother does all that, and he goes round once in a while and is the ideal parent.

'He used to leave me and go back to his parents when it all got to be too much for him. . . . he would walk out and I'd have to cope with Chloe on my own. Once he disappeared for a month. I had no money. I didn't know where he was. His parents would not speak to me on the phone. His father always hated me. They did not want us to get married.

'I was seventeen, my parents both dead, who could stop me? And he was eighteen. I thought that I could give myself the family that I had lost. But I lost everything, didn't I?

'I think that his parents were pleased when he went home, telling them tales . . . and then he would just reappear and the place would be filthy; Chloe not washed and nappies everywhere. He'd say it was like a pig-sty, but he did nothing to help. He went home complaining to his parents and had meals cooked for him, and his washing done, and got some sleep . . . then he would turn up here complaining. I couldn't manage on my own.

'I reasoned that if his mother looked after the baby, at least he would not keep coming back to me, there would be nothing to return for. He could stop pretending that we were a couple, or that we still lived together. His mother was always asking him to take her grandchild to her and let her rear it properly. In the end I let him. I was in danger of doing Chloe harm, I really was. But I didn't think that it would all go through court. I never imagined that they would do that. It sounded then as if it was all my fault, but it was both of us who couldn't cope; only I was in it on my own.

'He was awarded custody on the proviso that his mother brought up the child. I was relieved, because it meant that Chloe would get a home. Neither of us could give her one.

But it was not fair the way they made me out to be the one who had failed, I had no family to fall back on to.

I had no one to give me support the way he did. Then they had her made a ward of court.

'I would not try to take Chloe back after all this time. Why can't they see that I wouldn't do anything that might unsettle her? God knows, she's had a rough start. I wouldn't do anything that was unfair. All I want, is to see her from time to time. I want her to know who I am. That's not unreasonable, is it? I'm a stranger to my own child. For all I know, they could have told her that I'm dead.'

She put the forgotten cigarette to her lips and inhaled with a jerking movement of her head. She breathed in the dregs of tobacco and stubbed out the remaining stump. No sooner had she performed this action, than she had already forgotten what she held in her hand. Her eyes were dreamy and I knew that she was with Chloe.

It seems a long time ago, that evening. Now Celeste is a friend, we no longer have to pretend that there is some other reason for us to meet.

Now she is proud of her daughter's progress at school. Occasionally she is allowed to phone her mother-in-law for news. There are the times that Celeste is excited and I see her with a smile, that does not fade but remains, when she has a pleasant memory which nothing can remove. Like the time she spilt hot milk on her foot, it was as if she did not feel it. She is like someone who has suffered enough pain and cannot register more. That day she walked awkwardly, avoiding that foot making contact with the floor, but she had heard news of Chloe and her senses were glutted, unable to let pain through. In her eyes was a reflection of her daughter, whom she had heard was growing her hair, in order to put it in plaits.

Celeste contrives to see her child without being seen. She shops in the vicinity of her daughter's school, around the time it lets out, but she is careful to remain hidden or

Chloe, in her childish way, might mention to her grandmother that there is a strange woman always standing outside the gates, who does not speak to anyone but just watches. Celeste waits at bus queues, and looks in shop windows where she might see her child reflected from across the street. She controls the impulse to rush up to her, to touch her, and she won't allow herself the luxury of imagining that one day she might speak to Chloe. She knows it is an impossibility.

Recently Celeste was excited. She had seen Chloe again after the gap of the long, summer school holidays.

'Her hair is almost down to her shoulders, it's grown so long and thick!'

She came into the house. She had taken to dropping in on me to check how I was. I was in the last stages of pregnancy, lumbering and awkward, scared to go far in case anything started.

'Your eyes are bloodshot,' she said when she saw me close up. 'You must be due.'

Unlike everything else, this was one instinct that she was confident of.

'I was just like that, my eyes got terribly red before I went into labour.'

She placed a hand on my belly, firmly. 'It's solid,' she laughed. 'It's going to be enormous!'

We both started to laugh uncontrollably with nerves for the event. I was anxious, as all mothers are, that their child should be born safely. I asked her what her labour had been like, wanting to know if it hurt, what was it like? I had never asked her such a direct question about her daughter before. Celeste took her time answering and shocked me when she talked because I realized that she was not referring to Chloe, but to another child. Now I think that she was equally shocked because she had not intended to speak about this experience, and she stopped herself in time, telling me the rest of the story after my child was safely born, for this one had died.

194

My son was a robust and baldy six weeks old when Celeste finished what she had started to tell me. It was with great control that she revealed how she had felt nothing the first time. She was fifteen and not ready.

'I was no mother, the idea was ludicrous. And in some way it let me survive the ordeal, because when the baby was born dead, it was as if she had never been there. I had not accepted that I would have a baby, so in a callous sort of way I did not suffer the loss. Does that seem hard to you? I wonder if self-survival makes us so?'

She looked at me, and her face changed, warming with a smile that started far back in her memory and slowly showed itself.

'Let me tell you about Chloe.'

Then she had felt everything that she was expected to. Everything came together, everything felt right, and she held her daughter in her arms and sobbed with relief, and knew that she was part of her.

'I sat up on the delivery bed with tears pouring down my face, asking the midwife over and over if this one was really here to stay. They must have thought I was crazy, but I could not believe that I should be lucky and keep my child.'

She looked at me and tried to laugh at the memory of the surprised midwife and the young girl, unable to believe her luck, because she held a living child. There was silence, even my son seemed to sense it and became still in my arms. Celeste lit a cigarette.

'Maybe I'm not cut out for it, this motherhood,' she said with a shrug of her shoulders.

It was only then that I started to understand her sadness. Celeste had allowed a tiny drop to spill over and I thought that I would drown in it. My hands began to shake. I clung to my son, there was nothing I could say.

Celeste inhaled slowly and blew the smoke out through her nose. She watched me through the curtain of tobacco.

She laughed the controlled laugh of someone who prefers to observe life.

I was guilty. I loved my child.

'Hey,' she said. 'It's a long time ago, and I've grown up now . . .'

But we both knew as we looked at each other that time did not heal. The doorbell rang. It was N. I was never so glad to see anyone or to break the mood that existed.

The following morning Celeste, N and I went over to Camden. It was, I remember, one of those spring days when the air is still harking back to winter, crisp and clear. We had to keep moving. I was concerned for the baby in its papoose. I tucked and folded the little blanket around him. He looked up at me and I'm sure he winked. I walked slightly behind the other two, feeling tired and burdened visibly, but free and happy. It made me laugh, here I was the symbol of the mother and ahead of me the young lovers, for Celeste was holding N's hand.

I watched them move into the crowd, struck by Celestes's youthfulness, and I kept hearing her tell me that she had grown up now. Celeste could sink into this crowd. Childlike, she seemed to take on its bright playful behaviour, borrow some aspect of that clear morning so that she could move around in it unobserved, while I struggled at odds with everything. At Camden Road we parted. Soon she would be indistinguishable from the crowd as we moved further away. Laughing, she turned back once to wave at me and as I returned the wave, she disappeared from sight.

I walked slowly back with my son, aware of feeding times and nappy changes, thinking that for Celeste it never ended, the silent motherhood which she carries around with her. Unlike a baby which finally walks on its own, Celeste's babies lodged in her memory, small and helpless. She was sentenced to be a ghost mother, an unholy ghost who had transgressed and for her mistake was being punished. I decided that there was no justice. No merciful, all-encompassing God would allow such suffering. There was no innocent party, only the punished. And I went home slowly, thinking how she had told me a long time ago that when Chloe heard about her mother, she probably understood that she was dead.

Katie-Ellen takes on the World

There was a hiss from the gas cylinder as I sucked in air to my dry lungs. I held the mask hard to my face. Sturdy clear plastic, not at all like the rubbery, foul-smelling masks the dentist used when I was a very small child. They, I remembered, had made me nauseaous and repeatedly sick long after the tooth was extracted, the ache removed. I used to dream about them and wake up choking. Those masks were soft and greasy. They sucked my face and swallowed me. I dreaded that descent into half-consciousness. I would struggle against it, kicking the dentist in his white coat. Once, I caught hold of my mother's hand so desperately that her ring finger came up in a bruise. I would wake up still screaming for the mask, which was long gone, to be taken from my face. All the way home I would vomit and days after, I would turn suddenly ashen, as the memory of that vile gas and rubber smell swept over me, making me retch and cry with revulsion.

This mask was different. I heard the gas cylinder hissing. I knew that I could put it down at any time. There was to be no sweep into sleep, no unconscious soft darkness enveloping me. No rest. It seemed strange to remember that my main concern when I went up to the hospital to look at the delivery rooms was not with birth itself, but with the use of those masks. They were the first things I asked about. The nurse had handed me one.

'You administer it yourself,' she told me, as I gingerly felt what she held out. It was clear transparent plastic and cold to the touch. It was much smaller than I expected, more of a mouthpiece. I felt my confidence rising.

'Why don't you have a go? Just to get the feel of it. It will put your mind at rest,' she said kindly.

'Relax and breathe deeply, holding it over your mouth.' She positioned it for me. 'There, now when you feel that you've had enough, just let it drop.'

I was in control, with relief I inhaled deeply. Easy, I thought as I took another lungful. Quite silly really to be so worried. It had a rhythmic quality which was comforting and enjoyable. I filled my lungs once more, triumphant in my ability. Wonderful! I breathed in, feeling euphoric.

The nurse's voice seemed to be coming from a long way off as though she was on the other side of the door. 'Just hold on to the window rails until the room stops spinning. You have to go easy with it.'

'They're always like this the first time,' a passing midwife said.

Now I was right in the centre of that first time. It was another person who once went to inspect the delivery rooms. That person had been detached, unable to believe that the groans she heard coming through the partition would one day be hers. She had not known when this strange act called birth would seize her, and she walked around the hospital beds with a nurse commenting on the curtains, the bright airy rooms, and talking about her length of stay with the confidence of one safe in the present, contemplating the future. But I had been dragged into the awful present. I heard the hissing sound of the cylinder as I held the mask to my mouth.

There was a distant roar like thunder and an echo in my belly. I was at the centre of a strange landscape which was moving me along. The entire world was responding to the faint sound like Lambeg drumming, with its steady warning in a constant beat, its air of patient threatening.

I found myself lying in what might pass for darkness. I must have slept or fainted because I saw how the light had changed. Now it was a soft half-light, surrounding me with shadows as people moved around the bed. Light came shyly from a window. As I watched, it tried to disappear. Hiding in its own grey rectangle of light, the glass held back the heavy air pressing against it. Air which would pour in and wrap its damp self about me. I would suffocate in such air.

I heard a woman's voice. 'Move over a bit, then,' it said.

The midwife was giving me instructions. I felt her hand as she placed it strongly on my shoulder. She put her other on my leg and pulled my knee out. 'Push against this.'

But then a huge tremor shook me and I was carried behind the dragging movements of my abdomen, riding in a huge surge which landed me like a great fish, pulled on to the trawler's deck, twitching with the hook deep in its throat.

'Push.'

My last breath came like a grunt before the stillness. I flopped on my side, gasping for air. I wanted to rest but the fish's tail lay twitching and the sickening momentum began again. I flipped and rolled, not quite human now, a breathing tribute to instinct which forced me. I had to trust, not guide. I floundered, overawed by my own stength.

'Push.'

My legs shook. I was colder than I had ever been. The dragging feeling started again. My back caved in, I thought I heard it snap. Nothing happened.

'You can do better than that.'

I had no sense of where my body started or stopped. I felt that it was everywhere, without boundaries. It flowed on and on. It had no end.

'You're not doing it the way you've been shown.'

I tensed. I used everything; my veins, my muscles, my heart, my arse, even my eyelids pushed.

I would never manage it. Motherhood was not for me, but for another woman. Holy Mother of God, ever a virgin, blessed art Thou amongst women, not this woman. I grabbed the midwife's hand and held it. In the distance, a voice said it would be a long time yet.

Bob was massaging my back with round continuous circles of anxiety. Round and round in a pattern of his own, tracing his hopes on to my flesh. Suddenly I loathed it.

'Stop it! I don't want to be touched!'

The monotonous gesture irritated me and now I hated the hand I had so earnestly seized. I let it go, and rolled away from touch.

I waited. I breathed. Waiting, I thought; let them do it, her and him. Let the midwife get up on the bed and bleed and have this baby. Let him do some pushing instead. What did they think they were up to, leaving me to do it all?

Hot with sudden anger, I said, 'Leave me alone.'

But I meant completely alone, not with this volcano waiting to explode inside me. Why couldn't they do something? They, and I, were useless. And as I realized this, saw how helpless were our gestures against this terrifying life that took me up to throw me down gasping, I heard the gas hissing and felt the strength of another movement which flooded into me and took me after it. I knew then that I would go on; despair was no match for it.

Voices came softly out of the shadows, coaxing, cooing, urging me onwards, supportive voices as the tide swept me up and crashed me down again.

'Don't push.'

I thought I had misheard.

'Don't push.'

There was no mistaking its cool authority.

Everything tensed around me. I fought against the next

urge and sickness swept over me. I resisted the awful pain. How long could I hold out?

I wanted to tell them what I was enduring, tell them that it was impossible, tell them that I must push, but I had no method of speech left. Nausea had robbed me, and all I sent out were moans and growls, pathetic as any animal in pain.

I struggled until the hurt dragged itself off, but I knew it lurked in the brightening room, waiting to kick.

'I can't do that again,' I told the midwife.

'You won't have to. You can push next time. You're ready.'

When the pain came back, I moved into it gladly. I moved it away and out. I felt relief and almost pleasure.

'One more!' the midwife said.

I made another effort and felt something drag, something hard. Bob's voice shot across the room.

'The head! The head's out!' and there was stillness in which none of us breathed.

As soon as I had the urge to push again, I did so, and felt at once the slippery, wet rush of my baby as she came into the world to lie warmly along my inner thigh. The nurse scooped her up and laid her on my breast.

I reached out and touched her carefully, stroking and exploring this new person who bellowed with healthy lungs, breathing on her own in the strange atmosphere, ruddy and drunk on oxygen. I stroked her downy back, with its soft whorls of hair, and rubbed her ears with their little tufts.

'In a few days that will be gone,' the nurse told me.

'We won't wash her face until the tear ducts open. Those marks will wear off.'

My daughter wore proudly on her crown, the blood streaks she had been baptized in.

I looked around me and noticed for the first time that the room was full of people. Some were crying.

'This is Katie-Ellen,' I said, introducing her.

Her mouth opened and her tiny fingers made gentle pawing movements. I whispered to her that she had taken on the world and as I held her fiercely to me, I felt her small strong life vibrate.

Also available from Minerva

Michelle Cliff

NO TELEPHONE TO HEAVEN

'One of the finest and most moving novels of the past year.

'In this tale of identity and nationhood Cliff evokes a Jamaica full of contradiction and complexity, a country where history and politics are played out in surroundings of overwhelming physical beauty. Slowly the Jamaican diaspora is revealed through the novel's main character, Clare Savage, whose family emigrates to the US when she is twelve . . . .

'Clare's emotional and physical journey back to Jamaica and a positive identification of herself as Jamaican takes the form of a fascinating voyage through the polarities and dualities of race and sexuality, the relationships between the first and third worlds and slavery and modern patterns of emigration. Cliff powerfully evokes the historical myths and truths of Jamaican and Black Americans, and the beauty and anguish of modern Jamaica'   *City Limits*

'Michelle Cliff is a remarkable author'   *Guardian*

'Vividly and passionately written'   *Financial Times*

'Potent and very moving'   *Sunday Times*

'Full of razors and blossoms and clarity'   Toni Morrison

'A novel of great beauty'   *Marxism Today*

Nawal El Saadawi

THE FALL OF THE IMAM

'This is a tale of women suffering under harsh Islamic rule, but it could be about women anywhere there is cruelty and bullying. This novel is unlike any other I have read, more like a poem or a lamenting ballad, with something hypnotic about it, with its rhythmic, keening language, returning again and again to the same incident, a woman killed in the name of religion by the men who have used her.

  'This is a wonderful book and I hope a great many people will read it'   Doris Lessing

'A study of the psychology of power that goes far beyond slogans'   *Books*

'Comparable to Marquez's *The Autumn of the Patriarch* for the way in which it finds vital metaphors to describe religions and political brutality, this is also a work which dares all in order to get important things said'
Literary Review

'Clear and impassioned'   *Times Literary Supplement*

'Brilliant . . . technically inventive, thematically stunning'   *City Limits*

'Calls to mind the fundamentalist country of Margaret Atwood's *The Handmaid's Tale* . . . an intense and vivid book'   Hilary Mantel, *Daily Telegraph*

Brenda Maddox

NORA

A Biography of Nora Joyce

Nora Joyce is commonly portrayed by the literary world as an illiterate, coarse chambermaid and no match for her husband's genius. This new and enthralling biography is the first full study of Nora's life before, with, and after James Joyce. Here she is revealed as devoted, passionate, eloquent, irreverent, long-suffering and a powerful influence upon her difficult and demanding husband.

Brenda Maddox also portrays Nora as Joyce's inspiration for several female characters in addition to Molly Bloom, and offers fascinating new insights into the relationship between Joyce's life and his work. In releasing Nora from the world of academic footnotes, Brenda Maddox has produced both a fine biography of a complex woman and a work which will inform and interest all Joyce readers and scholars.

'One of the finest biographies to have appeared for some years' *Irish Independent*

'Nora is a brilliant biography that radically alters our understanding. With all respect for Ellman's monumental work, Maddox's biography of Joyce's wife can now be recommended as the first book to read about Joyce himself' *Newsweek*

'This book is irresistible' *The Spectator*

'Essential reading' Anthony Burgess

'[A] remarkable portrait of what must be one of the strangest, most fruitful, evenly matched, and in the end for both parties most thoroughly satisfactory of literary marriages' *Saturday Telegraph*

A Selected List of Titles Available in Minerva

While every effort is made to keep prices low, it is sometimes necessary to increase prices at short notice. Mandarin Paperbacks reserves the right to show new retail prices on covers which may differ from those previously advertised in the text or elsewhere.

The prices shown below were correct at the time of going to press.

Fiction

☐	7493 9026 3	**I Pass Like Night**	Jonathan Ames	£3.99 BX
☐	7493 9006 9	**The Tidewater Tales**	John Barth	£4.99 BX
☐	7493 9004 2	**A Casual Brutality**	Neil Bissoondath	£4.50 BX
☐	7493 9018 2	**Interior**	Justin Cartwright	£3.99 BC
☐	7493 9002 6	**No Telephone to Heaven**	Michelle Cliff	£3.99 BX
☐	7493 9028 X	**Not Not While the Giro**	James Kelman	£3.99 BX
☐	7493 9011 5	**Parable of the Blind**	Gert Hofmann	£3.99 BC
☐	7493 9010 7	**The Inventor**	Jakov Lind	£3.99 BC
☐	7493 9003 4	**Fall of the Imam**	Nawal El Saadawi	£3.99 BC

Non-Fiction

☐	7493 9012 3	**Days in the Life**	Jonathon Green	£4.99 BC
☐	7493 9019 0	**In Search of J D Salinger**	Ian Hamilton	£4.50 BX
☐	7493 9023 9	**Stealing from a Deep Place**	Brian Hall	£3.99 BX
☐	7493 9005 0	**The Orton Diaries**	John Lahr	£4.99 BC
☐	7493 9014 X	**Nora**	Brenda Maddox	£5.99 BC

All these books are available at your bookshop or newsagent, or can be ordered direct from the publisher. Just tick the titles you want and fill in the form below. Available in:
BX: British Commonwealth excluding Canada
BC: British Commonwealth including Canada

Mandarin Paperbacks, Cash Sales Department, PO Box 11, Falmouth, Cornwall TR10 9EN.

Please send cheque or postal order, no currency, for purchase price quoted and allow the following for postage and packing:

UK	55p for the first book, 22p for the second book and 14p for each additional book ordered to a maximum charge of £1.75.
BFPO and Eire	55p for the first book, 22p for the second book and 14p for each of the next seven books, thereafter 8p per book.
Overseas Customers	£1.00 for the first book plus 25p per copy for each additional book.

NAME (Block Letters) ....

ADDRESS ....

....